D0065412

A LOVE FOR LEAH

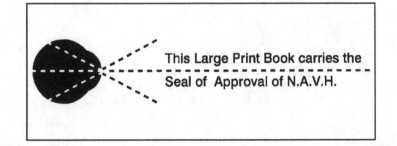

This Large Print Book carries the
Seal of Approval of N.A.V.H.

THE AMISH MATCHMAKER SERIES

A LOVE FOR LEAH

EMMA MILLER

THORNDIKE PRESS
A part of Gale, a Cengage Company

Farmington Hills, Mich • San Francisco • New York • Waterville, Maine
Meriden, Conn • Mason, Ohio • Chicago

Copyright © 2017 by Emma Miller.
The Amish Matchmaker Series.
Thorndike Press, a part of Gale, a Cengage Company.

LIBRARY OF CONGRESS CIP DATA ON FILE.
CATALOGUING IN PUBLICATION FOR THIS BOOK
IS AVAILABLE FROM THE LIBRARY OF CONGRESS

ISBN-13: 978-1-4328-4699-2 (hardcover)
ISBN-10: 1-4328-4699-X (hardcover)

Published in 2018 by arrangement with Harlequin Books S.A.

Printed in Mexico
1 2 3 4 5 6 7 22 21 20 19 18

Delight yourself also in the Lord and He shall give you the desires of your heart.

— *Psalms* 37:4

CHAPTER ONE

Kent County, Delaware
Spring

"What do you mean you won't marry me?" Thomas's eyes widened in disbelief as he stared at the young woman beside him. "Don't we go together like ham and cabbage? Bacon and eggs? Hasn't everyone been waiting for us to announce the wedding date?"

Ellie grimaced. "I'm sorry, Thomas. Truly I am." She sounded contrite.

He set her books onto the trunk of a fallen apple tree and they tumbled onto the grass. "You should be sorry," he said. "It's not easy for a fellow to propose to a girl. And when I do, you turn me down? It's humiliating."

It was late afternoon and the dirt path that ran from the Seven Poplars schoolhouse where Ellie taught, to Sara Yoder's place, where she lived, was deserted except for the two of them. The path crossed several Amish farms and this section wound through an apple orchard. The trees were bursting with new leaves and just beginning to bud from the branches on either side of the rutted lane. The only sounds, other than the thud of Thomas's accelerated heartbeat, were the buzzing of bees and the scolding song of a wren.

He scowled down at Ellie. "Why don't you want to marry me?"

"I should have never let it get this far." She looked up at him, her hands clasped together. "I knew we weren't meant to wed. But I like you and you're so much fun."

"I think you are, too. Isn't that enough? That we genuinely like each other and always have a good laugh?"

She shook her head sadly. "*Ne,* Thomas, it isn't enough for me."

In frustration, he yanked off his broad-brimmed hat and threw it on top of the scattered books. "I don't understand. I thought you wanted to be my wife."

"I never said that, Thomas."

He scowled.

She picked up his hat, brushed the leaves off it and handed it back to him. "I care for you, Thomas, but I don't want to have your babies, and I can't see us growing old together. We talked about this months ago. Remember?" Her blue eyes clouded with emotion.

"*Ya,* but I thought . . ." What *did* he think? She'd told him last fall that he needed to start walking out with other girls, but he hadn't, and the next thing he knew he and Ellie were running around together again.

"We're not a good match, Thomas. And if you're honest with yourself, you'll agree. I think what we have is . . ." Her brow furrowed as she seemed to search for the right word. "A convenient friendship."

"*Convenient?*" Needing to look her in the eye, he caught her around the waist and lifted her so that her small feet, clad in black leather lace-up sneakers, balanced on the fallen tree trunk. Ellie was a little person, and when she stood beside him, the top of her snowy-white prayer *kapp* barely reached the middle of his chest. After their first meeting he'd never thought of her as small, or different than any of the other girls he had walked out with. Ellie cast a big shadow.

Ellie's eyes registered a sharp warning. Putting his hands on her in such a familiar way was inappropriate, and they both knew it. At the moment, he was too upset to care.

A knot tightened in his throat. "Ellie, I don't understand," he said. "A convenient

9

relationship? What's that supposed to mean?"

His face must have shown how hurt he was because her features softened. "Maybe I shouldn't have said *convenient,*" she answered. "But you know exactly what I'm talking about. You and I run around together because it's easy. It's comfortable. But we're not in love with each other and you know it." With a sigh, she fixed him with a penetrating look. "Now stop feeling sorry for yourself and hear what I'm saying. It's for the best for both of us." She waited a moment, then added, "You know I'm right."

He glanced away, not ready to concede, no matter how right she was. He looked back at her and she offered a faint smile.

"Who told you to propose to me?" she asked him.

Flushing, Thomas felt a rush of guilt. She knew him so well. "My mother."

"Exactly." Ellie's eyes narrowed, making him feel as if he was one of her students who'd been caught staring out the schoolroom window instead of attending to his math.

"And what did your *mam* say?" Ellie demanded as she folded her arms. "Exactly."

He exhaled. "That it was time I had a family of my own." He ground the toe of

10

his work boot into the soft grass. "That you were a sensible young woman who would keep me in line, and I was foolish if I didn't pop the question before someone else did."

"Do those seem like good reasons?"

He gripped his hat so hard that the brim crushed between his fingers. He was devastated . . . sort of. "But we get along so well," he hedged. "And everyone says —"

"That because we have fun together, we should spend the rest of our lives as husband and wife?" She shook her head. "Not good enough. Not for me. Not for you." She was quiet for a moment and then went on. "And the truth is, Thomas, you're relieved. I can see it in your face. You weren't all that eager to tie the knot with me, no matter what your mother or anyone else said. Were you?" she pressed.

He wanted to protest, but Ellie was right. He was more surprised and embarrassed than brokenhearted. And he did feel a sense of faint but unmistakable relief. "No chance you'll reconsider?" he asked lamely.

She shook her head, took hold of his hand and jumped down onto the lane. "I'm not the special one for you, Thomas. If I was, you'd know it."

"You think?" He sank down on the log. "I'm not so sure. I've dated practically every unmarried Amish girl in the county and a lot of girls from other places. My buddies all found someone they wanted to spend the rest of their lives with, but not me . . ." He looked at her. "Maybe there's something wrong with me. Maybe I'm not meant to be married and have a family."

"Nonsense." Ellie picked up her books and brushed off the bits of grass that clung to the covers. "Your mother's right about one thing. It *is* time you married. Past time. I think your problem is that you don't know how to find the right woman. You're looking for the wrong things. You're looking *at* the wrong things, mostly pretty faces. Married life isn't just about fun and sweet smiles, Thomas."

"Now you *definitely* sound like my mother." He dropped his hat onto his lap, leaned forward and buried his fingers in his hair. The way Ellie put it, it made him sound shallow. And maybe there was some truth to the accusation. He'd been attracted to Ellie because of her cute figure, her pretty face and her sparkling personality. He liked pretty girls. And he liked to have fun. Was that so wrong?

"I sound like your mother because she's right. I'm right," Ellie insisted. "You want a wife and a family, don't you? You want to father children and live our faith?"

"Of course. I just don't —" He sighed. "I guess I don't know how to find that."

"Exactly. So what I'm thinking is that you need some help." She poked him with her finger. "You need someone to make a good match for you. You can't just look for a pretty face. You have to look deeper than that and find what's important in a partner. You need the matchmaker's help. You need Sara Yoder."

"You think I need a matchmaker?" he scoffed, meeting her gaze.

"Why not?" Ellie shrugged. "She's very good at it and it's not as though you're a hopeless case. You have a lot to offer a woman. You have a trade — two trades, if you count blacksmithing."

He frowned. "I'm a terrible blacksmith."

"Okay, but you're a decent rough carpenter. And you know something about farming. You have that promise of land from your grandfather, and you own a horse and buggy." She studied him carefully. "And you have a good heart and a strong back," she allowed. "You've never been afraid of hard work."

He flashed her a grin, recovering some of his equilibrium. "Not to mention that girls think I'm handsome."

"Humph." She puckered her lips. "Prideful, the bishop would say. And a show-off."

"I am not," he protested, rising to his feet.

"Red and blue blinking lights on your buggy?" She shook her head and sighed. "Thomas, I'm serious. You need to talk to Sara."

He thought for a minute. It had never occurred to him to hire the services of the local matchmaker. He'd always thought matchmakers were for people who couldn't get a date. That certainly didn't apply to him. He'd walked out with more girls in the last ten years than he could count. But Ellie was a sensible woman. Probably the most sensible he'd ever known. He knew he'd do well to take her advice. "Do you really think Sara could help me find a wife?"

"Absolutely. But pray on it. With your history, even Sara Yoder will need all the help she can get."

"Why do I think the two of you invited me here for something other than my rhubarb pie recipe?" Sara Yoder asked as she took a chair at Hannah's kitchen table. Hannah, her dearest friend as well as a cousin, had sent one of her grandsons with a note to ask if she could come over at four.

Since the weather was pleasant and the

14

two houses were less than a mile apart, Sara had walked. She liked being active. She was usually up by six and going until long after the sun had set. Not that it had done much for her figure. Despite her busy lifestyle, she remained hearty. She supposed it was partly that she loved to eat and partly because her mother had been substantial in size.

At the back door, Hannah's widowed daughter, Leah, recently returned from a long stay in South America, had taken Sara's denim coat and black outer bonnet and given her a big hug. Sara hadn't gotten a chance to get to know Leah yet, and she was pleased that she was there this afternoon.

"I'm so glad you could come," Hannah exclaimed as she dropped into a seat across from Sara. "We've been making vegetable soup and canning it. Cleaning out the cellar. Soon enough we'll have fresh vegetables again and I never like to save canned goods from one year to the next. I have a couple of quarts of soup for you. Too many to carry, but Leah can drive you home."

Leah wasn't Amish anymore, although in her plain blue dress and navy wool scarf she appeared so. When she'd married Daniel Brown several years earlier, she'd joined the Mennonite church. The Mennonites, close in belief to the Amish, were not as strict in daily lifestyle and permitted motor vehicles. Sara assumed that the small black automobile in the yard was Leah's.

Smiling, Leah brought a pitcher of cream and an old pewter bowl filled with raw sugar to the table. "Tea is such a treat," she said, joining them and pouring the first cup of tea for Sara. "I can't get enough of it. They have wonderful coffee in Brazil, but it was impossible to find decent tea."

All of Hannah's daughters were known for their liveliness and independence, but Leah was the one who residents of Seven Poplars saw as the most independent. After her marriage, Leah had left Delaware to follow her new husband to do missionary work among the indigenous people of the Amazon. There, in an isolated outpost, the young couple had operated a school, a store and a basic medical clinic. Then tragedy had struck. Leah had lost both her husband and her child to a deadly fever. Unwilling to leave her adopted community in need, Leah had remained more than a year until another team could be sent as replacements. Now, she'd returned to her childhood home to pick up the pieces of her life.

Leah might have been the rebel of the Yoder girls but, of all of Hannah's daughters, she was certainly the prettiest, Sara decided, looking across the table at her. Her red hair, blue eyes and flawless complexion made her a real beauty, more attractive even than Violet Hershberger, who was considered the cutest and most eligible girl in the county. But Leah's almond-shaped eyes held a depth of sorrow that gave her a fragility of spirit not evident in Violet or any of the other young women in the county. Leah seemed cheerful and strong enough physically. She laughed as readily as her sisters, but Sara could sense a vulnerability in Leah that tugged at her heart. It was obvious that she was still in pain from her loss, but Sara could see that she was making an effort to be a part of the world again. And she seemed to be succeeding.

Sara considered herself a sensible woman, one not easily swayed from the right path by emotion or hasty decisions. But she couldn't deny that she felt drawn to this girl and felt an instant desire to do whatever she could to help her. "It was nice of you to invite me for tea, but did you ask me here for the reason I suspect?" Sara asked.

Leah smiled and her cheeks blushed. "I think it's time I wed again and my family's in agreement."

"I'm glad you called on me, then. I've brokered a few Mennonite marriages, though you may have to be patient with me while I talk with some friends at the local church."

"Actually," Hannah said. "Leah has decided —" She broke off abruptly as her youngest daughter, Susanna, came into the kitchen with a basket of clothing she must have just taken in off the clothesline. Susanna had been born with Down syndrome and she and her husband David, also mentally challenged, made their home with Hannah and her husband Albert.

"The wind is picking up, isn't it?" Sara said to Susanna. She could smell the wholesome scents of sunshine and spring breezes on the clothes the young woman carried in the basket.

Susanna, red cheeked and beaming, nodded. "*Ya.* Almost blew me over."

"*Ach,* Susanna. You're about to lose your scarf." Hannah rose and went to her daughter, untied the navy cotton scarf and retied it in place over her daughter's braided and pinned up auburn hair.

"*Danki, Mam.*" Susanna giggled, her round face creasing into folds of pleasure. "As soon as I . . ." Susanna's forehead crinkled as she struggled to find the right words and pronounce them correctly. "Fold the sheets," she managed. "David's gonna show

18

me new kittens in the loft. He said 'Susanna, you help name them.' " She nodded excitedly. "They need names!"

"That sounds wonderful," Sara exclaimed, and then waited for Susanna to take her leave. Sara didn't need to be reminded not to speak of matchmaking business in front of Hannah's youngest. As delightful as Susanna was, whatever she heard, she repeated. It was impossible for Susanna to keep a secret. Arranged marriages were confidential between the candidates and the matchmaker, not food for neighborhood gossip.

Hannah took the laundry basket from her daughter. "Would you like me to help you fold? We'll take these sheets upstairs and put them away and then you can go and see the kittens."

"Ya, Mam." Susanna giggled again. "I'm gonna see the new kittens. We're gonna name them, me and David. I love David."

Hannah smiled lovingly. "I know you do. Now come along."

Leah waited until her mother and sister were out of the room before adding more tea to Hannah's cup and her own. Then she took her cup in both hands, gazed down into the swirling liquid and said, "I want to marry again, Cousin Sara." She sighed. "It's

19

been more than a year since I lost my Daniel and our little one and . . . I'm the kind of person who needs to be married. It's what God has always wanted for me." Her eyes teared up. "I want a husband and children." She looked up, unashamed of her tears. "Can you help me find a husband?"

Sara leaned forward. "Of course. As I started to say, my contacts among the Mennonite faith are not as extensive as —"

"Oh, I'm sorry," Leah interrupted. "I didn't make myself clear. I mean to return to the Amish church. I became Mennonite for Daniel, as was right. I believe it was God's plan for me at the time. And now, I think He means for me to accept the Amish way of life again."

Sara reached for a sugar cookie on a blue-and-white plate. "I assume you've considered this carefully? You've lived with many conveniences since your marriage. Are you sure that you can live Plain, as you did as a child?"

Leah didn't answer at once, and Sara liked that. This was no flighty young woman who chose first one path and then another on a whim. Sara nibbled at the cookie and sipped her tea.

"I've thought of little else since I left Brazil," Leah said finally. She offered a half smile. "I loved my husband. I've mourned him with all my heart. I think I will grieve for him until my last breath, even though I know he's in heaven. Grieve for myself, I suppose. But ours was a good marriage, a strong one, and I want that again. I'm young enough to bear more children, as many as God will send me, and to marry again just seems . . . right."

"Children are our greatest blessing," Sara said. She had never been fortunate enough to have a child, but she had loved many children and hoped to love more. Why God chose to not give some women children — or to take them away — she would never understand. "The ways of the Lord are often a mystery to us, aren't they?" she murmured.

"Ya," Leah agreed. "I thought I would lose my mind in those first months after I lost them. I know I shed enough tears to raise the level of the Amazon River, but, fortunately, I had our work. We had a small school and Daniel's clinic. He had been a nurse and I learned so much from him working at his side. After he was gone, there was no one else to help and I had to make do." She looked up and Sara gazed into the depths of those cornflower-blue eyes. "I delivered babies, sewed up knife wounds

and set broken arms and legs. I was too busy to think much about what I wanted for myself when I could come home."

"But you knew that you wanted to come home to Seven Poplars?" Sara asked.

Leah nibbled absently at a knuckle. Her hands were slender, her nails clean and filed. They were strong hands to go with her strong spirit, Sara thought.

"There was no question of my staying in Brazil as a woman alone. I wouldn't even have remained there as long as I did, but there was unrest. Trouble between the lumber contractors and the native people. And there were floods. They were so bad that our clinic was cut off from the nearest town for quite some time. It wasn't safe for a new team to come in. It was a blessing, really. I had a chance to say my goodbyes and see the school and clinic put in good hands before I left." Leah shook her head. "But I won't bore you with my memories. If you think you can help me, then I want to tell you what I require in a husband."

"I could never be bored with tales of your experiences in Brazil," Sara assured her. "But it would be helpful if you tell me what your expectations are in a husband."

Leah steepled her hands and leaned forward on the kitchen table. "First, he must be Amish, of strong faith and respected in the community. I would prefer a mature man, a middle-aged widower, someone who may already have children. How old doesn't matter, so long as he isn't too old to father children."

Sara pressed her lips together to keep from smiling inappropriately. This adventurous child of her cousin was certainly outspoken. Whether it was her nature or a trait she'd picked up in her travels, Sara wasn't certain. It was all she could do to not show her amusement. "You're still a young woman," she said. "Not yet thirty. Are you certain you wouldn't prefer a younger bachelor?"

"*Ne*. I'm sure of it," Leah said firmly. "I've been the wife of a young man. I married for love. I'll never have that again, and I know that. I'm a realistic woman, Cousin Sara. I know that affection and respect may lead to a different type of love someday." She met Sara's gaze. "I want someone different for a second husband, someone I'll not ever compare to my Daniel."

Sara nodded thoughtfully, and while she didn't know that she was in agreement, she certainly understood what Leah was saying. "Do you have a choice of occupations?" she asked. "Farmer? Carpenter?"

"It matters not. I'm used to making do

with few material goods. I ask only for a husband who isn't lazy and will be a good example for our children. He must know how much I want more children." Leah's voice took on a breathy tone. "I could not bear it if I never rocked another baby in my arms or woke to see my precious child's shining face beaming in wonder at the new day." She inhaled deeply. "So you see, it might be best if my husband-to-be already has children. I can adapt to any personality, but he must be someone who will welcome children and not treat them harshly."

"Or treat you harshly," Sara suggested.

Leah shrugged. "I can accept whatever the Lord sends me. I'll be a good and dutiful wife, so long as he knows that my children must come first. My Daniel was an indulgent father. He adored our . . ." Tears glistened in her eyes again. She looked down, took a moment, then looked up at Sara again. "I want to be sure I'm being clear, Cousin Sara. What I want is a marriage of convenience, a union entered into for the purpose of forming a solid family. I'm not afraid of hard work, and I'll be the best wife and helpmate I can. But I need a sensible man, a practical man who doesn't expect more than I can give." She hesitated. "Because part of me died in Brazil, Sara.

24

All I can do is go on with what I have left."

"You don't believe in the possibility of a second love?" Sara asked gently. "Not when you see how happy your mother is with Albert, after the death of your father?"

"I'm not my mother," Leah replied, sitting back in her chair. "I honor her, and I love her, but we are not the same. She and my father had many years together and time to form many memories. Daniel and I . . . It went by so quickly. Too quickly."

Sara considered the young widow's words. "Wouldn't your Daniel want you to be happy?"

"Of course." Leah smiled through the tears. "But I know myself. I know what I want. Offer me no lighthearted, carefree noodle-heads. I'm seeking a sober and steady husband, one with gray in his hair, who knows what it is to suffer loss. Can you find me such a man?"

Sara reached across the table and took Leah's hands in hers. "I will do my best to find what you need in a husband. But you must remember, I can't promise you children or happiness. We are all in God's grace and we cannot see the path He plans for us."

"I understand," Leah agreed. She squeezed Sara's hands and then pulled free.

"And I was hoping that you would have room for me at your house. Where I could stay."

"Certainly," Sara agreed, genuinely surprised by the request. "But what about your mother? Surely, Hannah must want you here with her."

"I don't think that would be best," Leah said firmly. "You know my mother. She'd want to put her spoon in my soup pot. I love this house and I love my family. But I'm not ready to fall into the habit of being a dutiful child again. You know exactly what I mean. I'm sure you've seen it before. A young widow returns home to her parents' house and the next thing you know, twenty-five years have passed and her mother is still cooking her supper and hanging out her laundry. No. I'll come to your home and put myself in your capable hands."

She rose and picked up her teacup to carry to the sink. "Find me a husband, Cousin Sara."

CHAPTER TWO

Leah drove her little car slowly down her mother's driveway, savoring the familiar sights of green fields, grazing cows and her brother-in-law plowing with a four-horse team. Beside her sat Sara, several quarts of vegetable soup in a basket at her feet.

"It's so strange to be back in Seven Poplars," Leah said as she came to a stop at the edge of the blacktop and looked both ways for traffic. A buggy passed the mailbox, and several automobiles approached from the opposite direction, so she waited until it was safe to pull out. "One minute I feel like an outsider, and a few minutes later, it's as if I never left home."

"For me, it's much like that, too," Sara agreed. "I haven't been in Delaware that long, but most of the time, I feel like I was born and raised here. Your mother and I have been close since we were children, but I didn't know anyone else until I got here.

It was a pleasant surprise to find all of Seven Poplars so welcoming."

"I'm so glad." Leah smiled at her. Plump Sara's hair was dark and curly, her eyes the shade of ripe blackberries and her complexion a warm mocha. Although a generation older, Sara was a widow like Leah. And Sara had also made major changes in her life after she was left alone.

When it was safe, Leah turned onto the blacktop in her little black Honda and smiled to herself, suddenly glad she'd decided to put her future in Sara's hands. She instinctively felt she could trust Sara, maybe even more than she could trust herself right now, which was why she'd decided to hire a matchmaker to find her a husband.

"Do you have a preference on where you live?" Sara asked, breaking into Leah's thoughts. "Does it have to be in Seven Poplars, or just in Delaware?"

Leah nodded. "I'd love to stay in Seven Poplars, but I know that's not likely. Though maybe you'd find a man looking to relocate here. Anywhere in Delaware would be fine. I just don't want to live so far from my family and friends that I can't visit again. I missed them so when I lived in Brazil."

"I can understand why you'd want to stay

here. This is a special community. Still, many young women might wish that they had had your opportunity — to travel so far to another country," Sara observed. "To see so many different kinds of people and to live in a jungle."

"It was an amazing experience. I feel blessed to have served God as a missionary. I already miss the friends I made there." Leah's throat clenched as she remembered the Brazilians standing on the muddy riverbank to wave goodbye. Small Pio clinging to his grandfather's leg, gentle Caridade nursing her new baby girl, and the collection of village elders, all in their finest basketball shorts, rubber-tire flip-flops and feathered headdresses. And around them their most precious possessions — the beautiful children, shrieking with laughter, heedless of the ever-present dangers of poisonous snakes, caimans and piranhas in the swirling, dark water.

"Their lives are so different from ours, harsher, and less certain," Leah murmured. "I went to teach, but ended up receiving far more than I gave."

"And do you have a timeline in mind? How soon would you like to marry?" Sara asked pointedly.

"As soon as possible." Leah gripped the

wheel, confident in her response. "It's time I was married, and God willing, I want another child as soon as possible." It felt good that she could finally keep her voice from breaking when she spoke of being a mother again. God truly was good, and time, if it didn't heal wounds, made them easier to bear. "Is that a problem?" she asked Sara.

"Not at all," Sara answered warmly. "You're past the mourning stage of widowhood. At your age, most would agree, the sooner the better."

Leah nodded as they approached a tall Amish man striding along on the shoulder of the road. Recognizing him, she slowed and waved. It was her brother-in-law Charley's friend Thomas Stutzman.

Sara waved and then glanced back at Thomas as they passed him. "Wait! Stop the car."

Startled, Leah braked, looking anxiously to see if she'd barely missed some hazard. "Something wrong?"

"Ne." Sara shook her head and motioned toward the side of the road. "Pull over onto the shoulder, can you? We should . . . I want to give Thomas some soup for his grandparents."

"Of course." Leah pulled over and put on

30

her flashers.

Sara got out of the car and motioned to the man. "Thomas! Hop in. We have some soup here for your grandparents."

Leah watched in the rearview mirror as Thomas approached the car. He and Sara exchanged words, but Leah couldn't make out any of what they were saying. Then Sara turned back toward the car. "No more than you could have expected. Ellie's quite set in her ways," Sara said as she walked back to the car and opened the rear door. "Get in. Leah won't mind driving you home. You can hardly walk and carry quarts of soup down the road. But you're headed in the opposite direction. You weren't headed home, were you?" She gave a wave, indicating again that he should get in. "No matter."

Thomas, seeming to realize there was no sense arguing with Sara, folded his long frame and climbed into the back. His head nearly brushed the roof so he removed his hat and dropped it into his lap. "Leah," he said in greeting.

"Thomas." Her backseat was small, and Thomas had broad shoulders. He took up most of it, even before he removed his hat.

Leah had seen him at church services the previous week. He was Charley's age, older than she was, but he'd always seemed

31

younger. Her sister Rebecca had told her that Thomas was still unmarried, but walking out with the little schoolteacher. Leah wished her well. Thomas was a good guy, though not the sort of man she'd be interested in. Thomas was far too immature and happy-go-lucky to suit her. And too self-centered.

"Your mother lets you keep a car at her house?" Thomas asked, glancing around the vehicle as he put on his seat belt. "I know you Mennonites drive, but . . ." He didn't finish whatever it was he was going to say.

"We do drive." Leah put the car into gear and eased back onto the road. "This car belonged to my late husband's cousin. Ben moved to Mexico to serve as a missionary and he gave it to me."

"Hannah doesn't object to Leah driving." Her arms crossed, Sara looked over her shoulder at Thomas. "Leah's Mennonite sister Grace drives every day, doesn't she? And Leah's stepfather has his pickup for veterinary emergencies. Bishop Atlee approved." She chuckled. "Leah isn't a child anymore. She respects her mother, but she doesn't ask for permission on how to conduct herself."

"That's what I tell my mother," Thomas said. "About me."

Sara made a small sound of disbelief. "And how does that work?"

"Not very well."

"Didn't think so," Sara replied.

"Doesn't work so well with my *mam,* either," Leah said with a grin. "It's why I'm going to stay at Sara's." She kept her eyes on the road. "I'd be happy to drop the soup off at your grandparents'," she assured him, "if you're headed somewhere else?"

"I'm going to Sara's actually," Thomas admitted sheepishly. "I left my horse and buggy there. Ellie — she's my girl — *was* my girl — Ellie likes to walk home after school on nice days like this. I thought it would be a surprise if I walked over and carried her books home."

"Ach," Sara said. "And it was you who got the surprise, wasn't it?"

"Ya," he admitted. He exhaled and went on. "I asked her to marry me and she turned me down."

"I'm sorry to hear that." Leah glanced at Thomas in the rearview mirror again. He didn't seem all that upset for a man who'd just proposed to a girl and been turned down. Seemed more put out than anything.

"Tough to be told no, but tougher to marry the wrong girl," Sara observed. "No need for you to take it personal, though,

Thomas. Ellie's been saying for months how happy she is teaching at the school. You just weren't listening. You know the board wouldn't keep her on if she married. She likes her independence, our Ellie."

"I knew that she said that," Thomas said. "But how was I to know that she meant it?"

Leah turned into Sara's driveway.

"By tonight, everyone in Seven Poplars will know Ellie refused me," Thomas went on. "I'm going to look pretty foolish."

"Ne." Sara shook her head. "Not true. You're not the first one to be turned down in Seven Poplars and you won't be the last. But maybe this will teach you to listen to what a woman says. She told you she wasn't going to marry you. I heard it myself."

"Guess I should have listened," Thomas admitted.

"I do know a thing or two about compatible couples," Sara said. "Which reminds me. I'm giving a get-together on Friday night in my barn. You should come, Thomas. There will be eligible young women there. I want to have games, as well as food and singing."

He shrugged. "I'm not sure I'd be good company."

"Nonsense," Sara replied. "I could use your help setting up. And if you don't come, you'll just sit home feeling sorry for your-self."

"I suppose I could make the effort. If you need me, I could come for a while, just to help out."

"It will do you good. Take your mind off losing Ellie." Sara clasped her hands to-gether and turned to Leah. "And you should come, too. It should be a lively evening — you'll enjoy yourself. And you and Thomas can catch up."

Leah eased the car to a stop near Sara's back door and Sara handed Thomas two quarts of the soup from the basket on the floor beside her feet.

"Thanks for the ride," Thomas said, get-ting out on the driver's side, a jar in each hand. "And for the soup. I know my grand-parents will appreciate it."

"No trouble." Leah smiled at him, leaning through the window. "It's not as though I took you far."

He started toward his buggy, parked on the far side of the barnyard, then turned back to her. "It's good to have you home again, Leah." Then he grimaced. "That didn't come out right. I mean, I know that you'd rather not have . . . that . . ." He looked down and then up at her, meeting her gaze. "I'm really sorry about Daniel and your little one."

Leah was touched by the emotion she heard in his voice. "Please don't feel that you have to tiptoe around me. This is a new start for me. What better place than home, where I have so much support?"

"Ya," Thomas agreed. He stood there for a second, then offered her the handsome grin that Amish girls all over the county talked about. "Well, see you."

Leah turned in the seat to face Sara as soon as Thomas was out of earshot. "I hope you weren't thinking of Thomas for me."

"Nothing wrong with Thomas that a little attitude adjusting can't fix," Sara said, getting out of the car.

Leah shook her head. "I wasn't criticizing him. It's just that he's too young, too . . ." She shrugged. "I don't know. Not a man I could call *husband.*"

"Don't worry," Sara assured her, picking up the basket with the soup. "I think I know exactly what you need." She closed the door and leaned down to speak through the open window. "Which is why you should come to the frolic."

Leah groaned and rested her hands on the steering wheel. "It's been a long time since I was single. I'm afraid I'll feel out of place with the younger girls and fellows."

"You won't. I've invited people of all ages. And it will give you a chance to reacquaint yourself with the singles in our community. There's a vanload coming from Virginia, as well, so there will be plenty of new faces." She held up one hand. "I know, no Virginian, unless he's willing to relocate. I just mean there will be interesting people to talk with — men and women."

"*Mam* tells me that you've made a lot of good matches. Still, I have to admit that I'm nervous."

"You won't be alone in that, but we'll muddle through." Sara chuckled. "We should have a nice-sized crowd Friday night. And Hannah told me that you have a lovely singing voice. We can always use another strong voice. Would you like to come in and see the room I have for you? You can move in as soon as you'd like."

"I don't need to see the room. I'm sure it will be fine." Leah glanced in Thomas's direction as he untied his horse's tie rope and slipped on the bridle. "I think I'd like to come tomorrow, if that suits you."

"It suits me fine." Sara watched as Thomas climbed up into his buggy. "He's a good man, Leah. Don't sell him short."

Leah pursed her lips thoughtfully. "He

37

doesn't seem all that broken up over losing Ellie."

"Because she wasn't the right one for him." Sara smiled and held up the basket. "I do appreciate not having to cook supper tonight. Your mother makes good soup."

"I know," Leah said. "It was one of the things I kept dreaming about when I was in Brazil — my mother's cooking." She paused. "You don't think I'm rushing it, do you? You don't think it's too soon to look for a husband?"

Sara smiled kindly. "*Ne,* I don't think you are. It's only right that we grieve for those we've loved and lost. But it would deny God's gifts if you couldn't continue on with life. A new marriage will give you a new beginning. I promise you, Leah. I'll find someone who will lift the sadness from your heart."

"It's what I want, too," Leah agreed, starting the engine of the little black car. "God willing, we can do this together."

Thomas stepped into the kitchen of Sara's hospitality barn. Bright lights illuminated the immaculate food-preparation area. The kitchen wasn't large, as Amish kitchens went, but it had a propane-powered refrigerator, double sinks, a freezer, a commercial

38

stove and new butcher-block counters. Leah was the only one there, and she was busy making sandwiches.

"Hey," Thomas said. He leaned jauntily against the double-door refrigerator. "Could you use some help?"

"Thanks, but I'm almost done." Leah deftly spread some of her sister Ruth's famous horseradish mustard on a slice of homemade rye bread and stacked on ham, cheese and pickles. "I thought Sara had too much food, but apparently not." She chuckled. "A hungry bunch, those Virginians."

"Probably the long ride. They're staying over until Monday. Fred Petersheim told me that there's talk they'll come quarterly. He's the short, gray-bearded farmer you were talking to."

"Ya." Leah nodded. "He talks a lot."

Thomas grinned. "About his Holsteins." Thomas had noticed that the older man had cornered Leah earlier in the evening. "He told me he lost his wife last winter. Does he have children?"

"Six, but two are grown and out of the house," Leah responded. "The rest are girls."

"He seems like a respectable man. I doubt Sara would invite him if he wasn't." Seeing that there were dirty dishes and silverware in the sink, he rolled up his sleeves, washed his hands and began to run warm water over the dishes. "I may as well wash these up," he said. A dishwasher was the one appliance Sara didn't have. With so much available help, she'd never seen the need.

"Are they still playing Dutch Blitz?" Leah placed the sandwich halves on a tray one by one. "I saw you won the first round."

"Lost the second," he said. "*Ya*, they're playing. Couples now." He reached under the sink for the dishwashing soap. "So, you've decided to let Sara make a match for you?"

Leah glanced over at him. "God willing. Sara seems pretty optimistic." She gave him a quizzical look. "Is she trying to find a wife for you?"

"I'm thinking about it. Ellie suggested it." He made a face. "I haven't had any success on my own."

Leah tried to open a quart jar of spiced peaches, but the lid was stuck. "Do you think you could open this?" Her vivid blue eyes regarded him hopefully. "Sometimes these lids are on so tight that it's impossible to get them off."

"Sure." Thomas dried his hands on a towel and took the peaches. The ring gave easily under his strength. Without asking,

40

he opened the other jar that she'd put on the counter beside the sandwiches. "Here you go."

"Danki."

Leah smiled her thanks and he was struck again by just how attractive she was. She didn't look like a woman who'd been married and had a child. She hardly looked more than nineteen. Before she'd wed Daniel Brown and gone to Brazil with him, most people said she was the prettiest girl in Kent County, Amish or Englisher. He and Leah had never dated because she was a lot younger than he was and didn't run with the same crowd. It was a shame she'd suffered such loss. But it did his heart good to see her here, still able to smile after all she'd been through.

Leah dumped the peaches into a blue-flowered bowl. "I'm surprised that you and Ellie are still speaking, let alone her giving you advice on finding a wife."

He grimaced. "I'll admit that I'm still smarting from the blow of her refusing me, but we're too good of friends to let that come between us."

"Sensible."

"She's special, Ellie. She'll make some man a good wife. I'm just sorry it won't be me."

"It says something about you, Thomas," Leah said, "that her being a little person didn't matter to you. If you had married, your children may have been short statured, like her."

"*Ya,* I did think about that. But it would have been in God's hands. And who's to say that being six feet tall is any better than being four feet tall?"

"Your parents didn't mind?"

Thomas returned to washing the utensils in the sink. "My father huffed and puffed, but my grandfather reminded him that he had an uncle who had only one arm. He said that Uncle Otto could outwork any man he knew. And once *Mam* and *Dat* got to know Ellie, it wasn't a problem anymore."

"Your grandfather sounds like a wise man."

"And a good one. He's been good to me. My brother will inherit my father's farm, but my grandfather has promised his to me. I was supposed to take up his trade, his and my *dat's,* of smithing, but I'm not sure it's what I want to do." He lifted a dripping colander from the soapy water and rinsed it under the tap.

"Were you trained as a blacksmith?"

He nodded. "*Ya.* I was, but I think everyone is beginning to realize I may not be cut

42

out for it. *Grossdaddi* has arranged for a new apprentice, Jakob Schwartz from Indiana. He's arriving tomorrow." Taking a clean towel, Thomas carefully dried the colander and put it in the cabinet under the sink. "Jakob's little, like Ellie, but *Grossdaddi* says he has the makings of a fine smith." He glanced at her. "You need the strength in the arms. Height doesn't matter."

Leah removed her oversize work apron. She was wearing a dark plum dress with a starched white Mennonite prayer *kapp.* "I suppose I should get these sandwiches out there."

"The platter is heavy. Let me," he offered.

"I can do it. I'm used to lifting heavy objects. Once, one of our parishioners brought home a quarter of a cow." Leah rolled her eyes. "I didn't ask where he'd gotten the beef. There was always a running feud between the farmers and the indigenous people." She picked up the tray.

"What was it like, living among them?"

"Wonderful. Awful. I never knew what kind of day we were going to have, one where nothing happened or one where the world turned upside down." She chuckled. "A fine missionary I turned out to be. I could never even pronounce or spell the name our people called themselves. They

43

are listed in our rolls as the St. Joseph tribe or the St. Joes."

"I'd like to hear more about them," Thomas admitted. "I'm curious as to what they're like."

She gave him a surprised look and set the tray down. "Really? You're one of the few to ask. Since I've come home, I mean."

He nodded. "*Ya,* I'm sure. But I've always been interested in the English world." He grimaced. "That didn't sound right, did it?"

She chuckled. "*Ne,* Thomas, it didn't. I wouldn't expect you to know, but I can't imagine a life more un-English than our village. But to them, it is all the world. Like us, most of the St. Joes want to remain apart, with their customs and their jungle."

He felt a flush of tingling warmth at the way she said his name, slow and sweet. He shifted his feet, suddenly feeling the conversation was getting too serious. "But what about that mysteriously acquired beef? Did you eat it?"

She laughed. "We all did. It was the season when protein is scarce. There were hungry people to be fed, so I asked the women to light the cook fires and we had a feast. Our refrigeration unit was very small, just used for medicine. Daniel was concerned that it would set a bad precedent, but I said, 'Eat

44

the cow or let her go to waste, and that doesn't sound very sensible.' "

"And did Daniel eat the meat?"

Leah shook her head. "It didn't keep me from enjoying every bite."

Thomas laughed, then grew more serious. "This has got to be hard . . . coming home. Starting again."

"Ya," Leah agreed.

Thomas's throat tightened. Leah had suffered a great loss. He had to admire her courage. "So I guess this —" he motioned toward the gathering beyond the door "— is as awkward for you as it is for me?"

"It is," she said. "I didn't want to come." She shrugged. "But Sara is very persuasive."

"Truer words," Thomas agreed as he picked up the platter of sandwiches. "So . . . back we go to meet Sara's likely candidates and hope for the best."

"Ya." Leah's smile was mischievous. "And be prepared to hear a lot more about Holsteins."

CHAPTER THREE

Thomas pushed open the sliding wooden doors to his grandfather's forge to catch some of the midmorning breeze. It was stifling inside, and he'd started to beat the last of the wrought-iron hinges into shape. Returning to his task, he used long-handled tongs to lift a smoking hinge into the sunlight to get a good look at it before plunging it back into the glowing coals.

His grandfather watched, faded blue eyes narrowed with concentration. *"Goot,"* he said. "A little more. Feel the shape in your mind, Thomas. Strike hard and true."

Thomas swung the hammer again and again. The shock resonated through his body, but he paid it no mind. He was used to it. He didn't mind hard work. It was *this* work he disliked.

Patience, he told himself.

Again and again he struck hammer to iron. Slowly the iron yielded to the shape he wanted. He knew it was good and he should have been pleased, but he took little pleasure in the forge. He much preferred digging in the soil or building with wood and brick. He'd been born to a family with a tradition of blacksmithing going back to the old country, but he had no heart for it. Never had.

"*Ya.*" Obadiah nodded. "*Ya.* That is the way. Was that so hard?"

Thomas placed the finished piece beside the others to cool and turned toward his grandfather. The gray-haired man held out a small bucket. Thomas took it, drank and then dumped the remainder of the cool well water over his head. It ran down his neck and shirt to wet his leather apron and forge trousers, but he didn't care. The pants and shirt would dry soon enough and both trousers and apron were scorched and riddled with holes.

His grandfather chuckled. "Always with you the heat, Thomas. The heat never bothers me."

And it never did. For sixty-five years Obadiah Stutzman had labored in a forge, and the flames and red-hot metal had only made him tougher. Past eighty now, his shoulders were still formidable and the muscles in his arms were knotted sinews.

Thomas loved him as he loved his mother and father. He couldn't imagine what life would be like without *Grossdaddi* watching over his shoulder, hearing the raspy voice hissing in *Deitsch,* "Strike harder, boy. Feel the iron." Thomas had always wanted to please him, but spending his life within the walls of this forge, he didn't know that he could do it.

Thomas walked to the open doorway and squatted on the hard-packed earth, letting the warm sunshine fall full on his face. He ran a hand through his damp hair and let his muscles rest from the strain of swinging the hammer.

In the distance, a calf bawled, its call quickly answered by the mother's deeper mooing. The farmyard stretched out in front of Thomas, familiar and comforting as always. Chickens squawked and scratched, earnestly searching for worms or insects. One hen was trailed by six fluffy chicks and a single yellow-and-brown duckling. Thomas smiled at the sight, knowing that when they came to the first puddle the foundling would terrify its adopted mother by plunging in and swimming. *Maybe I'm that duckling,* he thought, *always ready for fun, never quite fitting in or doing what I'm expected to do by my family.*

His grandfather came to stand beside him. "A sight you look," Obadiah said. "*Goot* thing your mother is to the house. Doesn't see you without a hat to cover your head in God's presence."

Thomas glanced guiltily at the wall where his straw hat hung on a peg. He never wore it in the forge for fear of it catching fire. *Grossdaddi* wore an old felt dress hat with the brim cut off over his thinning gray hair, but Thomas wasn't ready to be seen in such a thing, so he worked bareheaded.

"When do you expect Jakob to get here?" he asked. His father had told him at morning milking that the new apprentice was arriving today. He'd be staying with them in the big house.

"Anytime now. Hired a driver to bring him from the train station in Wilmington."

"I liked Jakob when I met him. I hope he works out," Thomas said. "Hope he likes Seven Poplars."

"Be a change from Indiana," his grandfather answered. "You know those folks don't even have tops on their buggies? Winter and summer, no tops. Their bishops won't allow it."

"I'd heard that," Thomas said.

"How was your social last night? Too bad Jakob couldn't have been here in time to go

49

along," Obadiah said.

"It was fine. Good food."

"Any new girls catch your eye? Your mother said she spoke to Sara yesterday about possibly making you a match."

"*Ne.* No one in particular; I spent most of the evening talking to Leah Yoder." Thomas shook his head. "Honestly, I'm having second thoughts about this matchmaker thing. Don't see why we need to lay out the money. I've never had trouble finding dates."

Obadiah turned a half-bushel basket upside down, sat on it and took out a penknife. Absently, he began to whittle at a small piece of wood he carried in his pocket. They sat in silence for a few minutes and then his grandfather said, "People say Sara knows her trade. They say give her a chance, she'll find you a proper wife."

"Seems foolish, though, doesn't it? Having her find me a wife? When I could do it myself?"

"But you haven't." His grandfather sighed. "Thomas, what can I say? Time you grew up. Started working in the family business. Trouble is, you think you can stay free and single year after year. You like the pretty girls. I can see it. But when talk turns serious, you're off after the next one."

Thomas felt heat flush his face. "It's not like that. I thought that Ellie and me would . . ." He trailed off, not wanting to talk about Ellie. That was still a sore subject. "I'm not certain Sara can find me a match I'd be happy with. She wanted me to meet this woman last night — Hazel something or other. One of the ones who came up from Virginia in the van. Sour as an October persimmon. Little beady eyes and a mouth screwed up so tight I thought she didn't have front teeth until I saw her eating. I couldn't imagine looking at that face across a breakfast table every morning."

Obadiah chuckled. "So, not pretty enough for you?"

Thomas shook his head. "That wasn't it. Hazel would have been attractive if she hadn't been so ill-tempered. Not a good word to say about anyone or anything. One complaint after another. She even complained about the potato salad. Said she preferred German potato salad to Sara's and left it on her plate."

"One wasteful woman doesn't ruin the batch. You're being stubborn. Time you started walking out with a respectable girl."

"I thought I was when I was with Ellie. And you all liked her."

His grandfather ignored that and went on.

"Bishop Atlee asked me last week if you were planning on going to baptism classes. Way past time, Thomas. I'm going to retire in a few years. Don't know how much longer I have on this earth. I know I've always told you that I wanted to leave this farm to you, but you worry me. I'm starting to have second thoughts. Maybe you mean to drift away from the faith. Maybe you're too flighty to entrust our family farm to."

Thomas winced as if his grandfather had struck him. This was the first he'd heard of his grandfather's hesitation about leaving him the farm. Since he was a boy, he'd expected it would be his someday. His throat clenched. "That's up to you, *Grossdaddi*."

"You should be married. You should have married five years ago. I could have great-grandsons and granddaughters to spoil. I've stood up for you to your mother and father, took your side when maybe I should not have." He exhaled. "You don't give Sara a chance to find you a wife, I have to take it into consideration that maybe you've lost track of what's important in life."

Thomas opened his mouth to respond, but his grandfather's shepherd raised his head and let out a single yip, then leaped up and ran toward the house. Thomas heard the beep of a car horn and the dog began to bark in earnest. "That must be Jakob coming now," he said, rising to his feet.

"Must be," his grandfather agreed. "But you think on what I said. I'm worried about you, boy." He met Thomas's gaze. "Prove to us all that you are ready to take over this farm. Find a wife, get to churching and be quick about it."

Sara smiled at Thomas as they shook hands across her desk. "So we're in agreement. I'll make you a match. Keep an open mind, and I'm sure I can find someone who will suit you and your family."

It had been more than a week since Sara's barn social. Thomas had spent days wrestling with the idea of asking for help in finding a wife. He'd prayed on it, and he'd considered asking the bishop to add his name to the upcoming classes in preparation for baptism in the fall. But he hadn't been ready to take that step yet. One obstacle at a time. Maybe finding the right girl would erase the last doubts he had about a Plain life. As much as his parents wanted him to join the faith, they wanted it for the right reasons. It had to wholeheartedly be his choice, not someone else's. The Old Order Amish lifestyle was a lifetime commitment, one you were supposed to enter with joy.

Tonight, he'd come after supper, as Sara had asked. He hoped that he wouldn't run into Ellie or Leah. It wasn't that he was embarrassed about using a matchmaker. It was more that a man's personal business ought to be private. And what could be more personal than choosing a wife?

Thomas hadn't mentioned to Sara that his grandfather was threatening to leave the farm to someone else. The possibility of losing the farm hurt, but if Thomas hadn't thought that maybe his grandfather was right, he would never have agreed to make an official agreement with the matchmaker.

He started to rise from his chair, but Sara waved him back into his seat. They were in her office in her home, a spacious room with comfortable furniture, deep window seats and a colorful braid rug.

"Don't go yet," she said. "I have a fresh pot of coffee and a blueberry pie that's just begging to be sliced." She made a few more notations on the yellow legal-sized notepad and tucked the sheet into a manila folder.

"How long do you think it will take?" Thomas asked. He rested his straw hat on one knee and looked at her.

"Slicing the pie or finding you a wife?"

He grimaced, still not entirely convinced this whole matchmaker thing was a good idea. "Finding somebody for me."

"Actually, I already have someone in mind."

"Not that Hazel girl you introduced me to the other night," he protested. "I didn't care for her at all."

She chuckled. "Not Hazel. Funny you should mention her, though. She and Fred Petersheim hit it off. It seems he didn't care for my potato salad either."

Thomas laughed. "I thought it was great."

"I'm pleased. Now," she said, rising, "you make yourself at ease. I won't be a moment. How is it you like your coffee?"

"Sugar and milk. Two sugars."

"You like it sweet."

"*Ya,* I do. I could come out in the kitchen with you," he suggested. "No need for you to —"

"No. Stay where you are, Thomas." She walked from the room, closing the door behind her.

Thomas tapped the heel of one boot nervously. He glanced around the room. The pale blue walls were hung with cross-stitch family trees and several large calendars. One showed a farmer plowing with a six-horse team against a rural background.

Another showed a mare and newborn foal, the little filly tentatively trying out her new legs in tall clover.

In one corner of the room stood a battered green filing cabinet. He wondered if there was a manila folder in one of the drawers that would hold his future. It was exciting and a little frightening to put his life in Sara's hands. He was tempted to wander over and take a peek. He wasn't normally a snoop, but if he just —

The door opened and Thomas turned his head to see not Sara but Leah. She was carrying a tray with slices of pie and three cups of coffee. "Oh!" he said. "You startled me." He rose and hurried to take the tray, realizing that although he'd hoped they wouldn't run into each other this evening, he was pleased to see her.

"Sara asked me to bring this in," Leah explained with a smile. "She said she'll just be a minute." He put the tray on the desk, and she took a seat opposite him and motioned to the coffee. "Please, go ahead. It's nice and hot."

He noticed that she was wearing glasses. He didn't think that she had worn them at the barn frolic. But they did nothing to hide the intelligent sparkle of her bright blue eyes. Leah should have been as plain as a barnyard dove in her worn gray dress, apron and headscarf, but red-gold tendrils of hair framed her heart-shaped face, and merry dimples gave her a mischievous appearance.

He wondered if Sara could find him someone like Leah. But maybe not so pretty, he thought. Ellie had warned him that he needed to look beyond an attractive face and neat figure.

A minute or two passed. Leah cupped her coffee mug in her hands and inhaled the steam. She didn't speak, and Thomas realized that the silence between them wasn't awkward. Rather, he found it peaceful. Most girls he knew liked to fill every second with chatter.

He tasted his own coffee. It was good. He would have to ask Sara what brand it was. His mother was an excellent cook, but her coffee left something to be desired. It was either too weak or something. It never tasted as good as Sara's. This was hearty, with a brisk, bright flavor.

"I guess it was quiet in the jungle," he remarked. "No traffic, not many people."

Leah smiled and shook her head. "Not noisy like here in the States, but certainly not quiet. There were so many insects, buzzing, flapping, whirring. For the first month I was there, I found it hard to sleep. And the monkeys? Some kinds scream, others howl. They all chatter nonstop. And sometimes you'd hear a deep rumble, like a cough in the night. Iago said that when I heard that noise, I should stay inside the house or clinic hut because it was a leopard and I would make a fine meal for a big cat."

Thomas gave her a sharp look. "A leopard? Did you ever see one?"

"No, but Iago said that they came to our side of the river in the rainy season. One had killed a child from the nearest village two years earlier. He wasn't given to tall tales, so I believed him." She rested her mug on the wooden arm of her chair. "You would think him odd if you saw him. He wasn't as tall as me; he had a potbelly, and his hair was cut like a cap just below his ears. Even though he was a great-grandfather, his hair was still as black as soot and coarse as a horse's mane. Iago's tattooed face was wizened like a winter apple and his legs were bowed, but he was stronger than you can imagine. He was my dearest friend other than my Daniel, and I shall never forget him. Iago taught me so much about life. It was his wisdom and patience that made it possible for us to live and work among the St. Joes."

"I would like to have met your Iago,"

Thomas said.

"You would have liked him. He told such stories that I could listen all day."

"He spoke English?"

Leah chuckled and shook her head. "Only a little. His granddaughter translated for me, and Iago was a fine actor. He used such expressions and hand movements that it was easy to follow."

"Who was easy to follow?" Sara asked as she entered the room.

Thomas stood. "Leah was telling me about some of her adventures in Brazil. It seems she was nearly eaten by a leopard."

"I didn't say that." Leah laughed.

Sara took her place behind her desk and helped herself to a slice of pie. "Mmm. Coffee's still hot. Good." She motioned to the other plates of pie. "Well, what are you waiting for? It's for eating, not looking."

Thomas took a plate and handed it to Leah.

"I should leave you two alone," Leah said, rising, her plate in her hand. "If you and Thomas have business."

"We do." Sara wiped a drop of coffee from her lip. "And so do you and I." She glanced from one of them to the other. "What? You really haven't guessed, have you?"

"Guessed what?" Thomas asked. He

looked at Leah, who had sat down again, then back at Sara. "Wait. You don't mean —"

"*Ne,*" Leah pronounced firmly, looking at him and then at Sara, too. "Not Thomas. Not for me." Her cheeks took on a rosy glow. "It's nothing against you, Thomas," she hastened to explain, glancing back at him again. "But you're not what I —" She turned her attention to Sara again. "I was very clear what I'm looking for. An older man. Settled. With children."

Thomas shook his head, wondering what Sara could be thinking. "We've known each other our whole lives. You don't think —"

"Stuff and nonsense!" Sara interrupted him, seeming perturbed. "Listen to the two of you. Who is the expert here? I've made more matches than you can imagine, and I think I know my business. You're perfect for each other." She pointed at him with her fork. "You're badly in need of a wife, Thomas. And Leah doesn't want to leave Seven Poplars and her family. What could be a better solution?"

"But Thomas isn't . . ." Leah murmured.

"She . . . she doesn't —" Thomas struggled to find the right words. If she wasn't interested in him, he certainly wasn't going to be interested in her.

"Look. Either you have faith in me or you don't," Sara said crisply. "Leah, you wanted an arranged marriage, someone of the faith that your family would approve of. And Thomas, you've been hopeless at finding someone on your own." She fixed him with a determined gaze. "So here's what I propose. Six weeks of dating. That should give you each time to consider the pros and cons of the other."

"But I don't want to date Thomas," Leah insisted. "He's the last sort of man I'd want to marry."

Her words hurt him a little, and he felt his own ire rise. "She's not what I'm looking for," he blurted. "I won't consider —"

"Oh, but you will," Sara said rather firmly. "You will both agree to give this match a fair chance. Because if you don't, if you won't even open your minds to the possibility, then I'm not the matchmaker for you." She sat back in her chair, crossing her arms over her chest. "And I'll wash my hands of both of you."

CHAPTER FOUR

Leah didn't know what to say. She didn't know if she was more disappointed in Sara or upset with her that she would suggest such a thing. Hadn't she just told Sara the other day that Thomas was all wrong for her? A terrible match. Of course, he was a good person. This was awkward, so much so that she almost wished the floor would open and let her drop through to the cellar. Anything to get out of this chair and away from Thomas.

"Well?" Sara said. "Are we in agreement, Leah? Six weeks?"

"I . . . I'm just afraid it would be . . .a waste of everyone's time," Leah hedged. "Not helpful for . . ." Her fork fell off the plate. She grabbed for it and missed. The fork clattered to the floor leaving a trail of blueberry-pie filling across the hardwood. Her face felt warm; she knew she was blushing. She reached to pick it up but Thomas was quicker. He grabbed the wayward utensil and dropped it onto his empty saucer.

Leah seized a napkin off Sara's desk and wiped at the mess. It smeared and she got down on her knees to get the last of the blueberry smear.

Sara cleared her throat.

Leah got up hastily, crumpling the dirty napkin and shoving it into a spacious apron pocket. She glanced toward the door, wondering if she should make a run for it.

Sara folded her arms again and looked at Thomas. "What about you? Are you willing? Would you date Leah for six weeks?"

He started to rise and then settled back into his chair. "*Ya,* I suppose I could. I mean . . ." His tanned complexion flushed. "It's just that I wasn't expecting . . ."

"You can see that it wouldn't work," Leah blurted, finding her voice. "He doesn't want —"

"Nonsense," Sara interrupted. "What Thomas wants or doesn't want clearly hasn't been working, has it? That's why he came to me." She turned and their gazes locked. "And you came to me. You asked for my help. My opinion. And I'm giving it to you. My opinion is that you and Thomas may be a good match. An excellent match."

Sara steepled her hands and leaned forward, elbows braced against the desk. "And if nothing else, six weeks will give you time to settle in to Seven Poplars again. What is it the sailors say? Get your sea legs?"

Leah was in no mood for humor, but what could she say? She had hired Sara and she had put her trust in her abilities. And it wasn't as if she could go door-to-door knocking at farmhouses, asking if there was an eligible bachelor available. She'd wanted a matchmaker so that she wouldn't have to make a decision, so that the weight would be taken off her shoulders. Her plan was that whoever God sent, she would accept.

"I . . . I just . . ." Leah didn't know what to say.

"Come now, it's not as though I'm asking you to cry the banns next Sunday," Sara said. "And Thomas is an acceptable escort. You might have fun. And if the two of you go to frolics, singings, socials, who knows — you might meet someone you really like." She hesitated. "Humor me, Leah."

Leah looked at Thomas. "What do you think?"

"I see no harm in it." Thomas shrugged. "And it could be fun."

"Ya," Leah replied. "You *would* say that."

He chuckled. "Sorry. I do like having a

good time."

"Well?" Sara asked.

Leah looked from the older woman to Thomas and back to Sara. "At the end of six weeks, if we both feel the same way, will you find me the older widower I asked for?"

"Of course," Sara agreed. "And if I've made a mistake and wasted your time, I'll consider a substantial reduction in my fee for your new matches."

"Could we talk?" Thomas suggested. "Just Leah and me?" He glanced at her. "If you're agreeable, Leah?"

"*Ya,*" she said.

"Fine." Sara got up from her chair. "Take all the time you want. But I'll leave the door open, for propriety's sake." She paused on her way out. "You two need to trust me. I know what I'm doing."

"I wish I was certain of that," Leah admitted, once she and Thomas were alone.

"Want to sit down?" Thomas motioned toward the chair she'd vacated. "Talk about this?"

Leah nodded, taking Sara's seat, putting the desk between them. "I'm sorry about you being put on the spot this way. I had no idea that she was going to suggest —" she began.

"Me neither," he said, cutting her off.

"Sorry, I didn't mean to interrupt. I just don't want you to think I was in on this."

"I know you weren't. It's fine. This is just so —"

"Awkward," he finished for her.

"Ya," she agreed, and found they were both chuckling as though they shared a joke. And perhaps they did. Sara's ruse. "I suppose we're stuck with this," Leah ventured.

"Ne. Not if it doesn't suit you. If you find me that . . ." Thomas seemed to search for a word. "Distasteful."

Leah shook her head. "It's not that. I like you, Thomas. You're a good man. Just not . . ."

"What you were looking for," he supplied. "I understand."

"I'm glad someone does." She nibbled at her bottom lip. "I thought it would be easier than this."

His dark eyes lit with humor. "It would have been if I'd taken a fancy to Hazel."

"And if I liked Holsteins more." She returned Thomas's smile with one of her own. She felt her annoyance slipping away. He was sweet. What harm could it do to humor Sara? It would only be for six weeks, and then she would get on with the process of making a serious arrangement. "I think we should just give in gracefully," she admitted. "I think Sara has us in a corner."

"Actually," he said. "You might be doing me a favor. It will give me some time to get my family off my back." He arched a brow questioningly. "Are you in?"

Leah nodded and offered him her hand. "I think we have a deal. Six weeks and no hard feelings when we break it off."

His stood again and strong fingers closed around hers as he reached across the desk to shake on it. "Six weeks," he echoed quietly. "We walk out together, have some fun, and everyone is satisfied."

"And then we get on with our lives," she finished.

"*Goot* enough." He squeezed her hand and then released it. "So, will you let me walk you home after church services tomorrow?"

"Tomorrow?" Her eyes widened in surprise. "Are you sure? So soon?"

"*Ya,* tomorrow," he answered steadily. "Why not tomorrow? We've made a bargain, haven't we? When I agree to something, I keep my word."

"All right," she said, smiling at him again. "Me, too."

"A good sermon," Leah said. "Not too long."

Thomas nodded. "Your sister's husband is a good preacher. When Caleb first came to Seven Poplars, we thought he might not be a good fit, but we were wrong. We like him." He grinned at her. "Partly because he doesn't speak to hear the sound of his own voice."

"But what he said was powerful," Leah replied. "A good preacher doesn't need to shout to deliver God's message."

"*Ya,* I agree." Thomas bent to pick up a stick lying on the edge of the blacktop and tossed it into the woods. "When a sermon is too long, a man's thoughts drift. I like the short ones best."

It was late afternoon and they were on their way back to Sara's house after worship. Ahead of them, a few hundred yards, walked a young family: a mother, father and three children. Some distance behind them, another couple strolled. Buggies passed at regular intervals, followed by an occasional automobile or pickup truck, but this was a narrow country road with little traffic other than locals, a safe road for walking.

The Kings' farm, where services had been held today, was two miles from Sara's, but the weather was mild and the spring sun warm on his face — so warm that Thomas looked overdressed in his coat and vest. She suspected that he would rather remove the coat and walk home in shirtsleeves, but it wouldn't be proper on the Sabbath. Thomas seemed *fast,* almost reckless at times, but he wasn't outright rebellious.

Leah was comfortable enough in her gray cotton dress and black leather oxfords. She considered herself a good walker, and although Thomas's legs were a lot longer than hers, she had no trouble keeping up.

Thomas groaned and patted his stomach. "I think I might have had one too many helpings of Anna's shoofly pie."

"Greedy. You should have stopped at one slice."

He chuckled. "I thought it was delicious, but I couldn't be sure until I ate a second piece."

"Three," she reminded him. "You had three slices."

"Small slices," he admitted, and laughed with her. "This isn't so bad, is it? Walking out with me? Unless you'd rather be driving."

She shook her head, thinking of her little black car parked behind Sara's chicken house. "I don't mind walking," she answered. "It's good exercise. We walked all the time in Brazil. There are no roads where we were. It was travel by boat down a river, fly or walk. Mostly, we walked. It could take hours or days to get to a sick patient or a village where Daniel was preaching."

"You walked for days through the jungle? Weren't you afraid?"

"Sometimes. Not often. Most of the tribes-people are quite shy of strangers. We always traveled with a guide, someone who could speak their language. Usually, we were welcomed into their villages and treated as honored guests. If I was afraid of anything, it was the snakes." She shuddered, just thinking of them. "There are several that are extremely poisonous. Deadly, even with modern treatment. I never learned to lose my fear of snakes."

"You said there were lots of insects. Mos-quitoes?"

"Far too many. And some carry diseases such as malaria and dengue fever."

"And here I thought Delaware mosquitoes were bad."

"They can be." She rubbed her arms. "Don't remind me. They aren't out yet, and it's much too pleasant to think about them."

"August was bad last year. We had a lot of rain and they hatched by the millions. Huge and hungry."

"Lovely," she said. "I can't wait."

Thomas chuckled. "Well, I guess we raised

a few eyebrows when we left the Kings' together."

"I'm sure we set them all atwitter," she agreed. She was surprised at how much she was enjoying the day. She'd expected having Thomas walk her home from church would be awkward, but she found him comfortable to talk to. He had an easy laugh, and it was nice having him beside her.

"My grandfather saw us and nodded his approval." He made a reluctant sound. "I feel a little bad about deceiving him, letting him think that we're walking out together."

"But, we are, aren't we? We did promise Sara a six-week trial."

"I suppose you're right," Thomas said. "It isn't really a ruse. Not if we do date like we promised. Even if we both know that this isn't going to work out."

"Exactly," she agreed. "You know, honestly, I can't see why you haven't found someone. There's nothing wrong with you that I can see."

"I'm glad to hear that."

His tone seemed a little stilted. "Don't take it personally, Thomas. And who knows? Maybe Sara will prove us wrong. Maybe we'll fall madly in love."

He chuckled with her. "Right."

Leah stopped walking and looked up into his face. "But I warn you, you'll have to be careful what you say. My sisters are relentless. They'll try to drum every bit of information out of you. They'll interrogate you just like one of those detectives on the television shows."

"Have you watched a lot of television?"

"*Ne.* Not much, but you can't help but see it now and then when you travel a lot."

"I suppose you miss it now that you're living with Sara."

"*Ne.*" She shook her head. "I don't. Mostly television is reporters shouting about fires or shootings or some movie star's latest scandal or people running around and blowing up things. Life is better without it."

"I suppose." He took her arm, guided her off into the grass as a truck passed and then released her.

Leah felt a warm rush of pleasure. How long had it been since she'd felt a man's touch? It felt good, and the realization made her wonder how she could so quickly forget that she had once been a married woman. And now was Daniel's widow.

Subdued, she turned the conversation to Thomas after they had walked a short way. "Your family must be eager for you to settle down and start a family. As much as my

72

family wants me to marry again."

"You could say that."

When she didn't comment, he found himself telling her about the conversation he'd had with his grandfather about the farm. "I wasn't expecting that," he concluded. "I never thought that he'd threaten me about the land."

"What will you do?" she asked.

"I'm not sure. I wanted to shout back at him. To tell him that he couldn't pressure me into marrying just anyone. But I bit my tongue. I just . . ."

She nodded. "I understand. It isn't easy with those we love. They want to help, but they cause more problems. It's one reason I decided to stay at Sara's. *Mam* pities me because of what happened to Daniel and our baby. She wants to protect me and to tell me what to do with my life at the same time." Leah flashed a brilliant smile. "But I'm not letting her get away with it."

"Still," he said, "you must have . . ." He wanted to say *suffered* but, instead, just trailed off. "It was a great loss," he finished.

Leah swallowed back the surge of hurt that threatened her peaceful day. "I have to believe that they're in a better place. It helps that I know the two of them are together in the Lord's care. And that if I live a good life

I'll see them again." She forced a smile. "I know that. Just as I know that my Daniel would have wanted me to live on, for all of us."

"*Ya,*" Thomas said. "I see the wisdom in that." He touched her arm lightly. "I think you are a brave woman."

She shook her head and chuckled wryly. "Not brave. Just trusting that God has a path for me and that all I have to do is to try and find it."

They walked a little farther in silence, and then he said, "You make me realize that my problems are small."

"Finding a wife?"

"That is an obstacle. But it's more than that. My grandfather, my father, my whole family expect me to follow tradition and become a blacksmith. But it's not what I want. It's not how I see my life. Does that make me selfish?"

She stopped and looked up at him. "You shouldn't feel guilty because you don't want to be told what to do for a living. My family certainly didn't want me to marry a Mennonite and go to Brazil as a missionary. But it was my choice. Surely, each person has the right to choose what's best for them."

"*Ya.* It's what I think, too. But it's hard to disappoint my grandfather and my father. It

74

means so much to them."

"But you are your own man, Thomas. You should be. Otherwise, you're just a shadow of them."

He smiled. "It doesn't sound so bad when you say it that way."

"So what would you do with your life, if you could choose? Sara told me that you work construction sometimes and that you help on your grandfather's farm. Do you prefer one or the other? Who knows? Maybe you haven't found your place yet. Maybe that's why you haven't settled down."

"I do like farming, but not the way my grandfather wants me to farm. Corn. Soybeans. Hay. The same old crops, fields of them. Commercial fertilizer. I don't think that's the way to go. If I could do anything, I'd like to start small, raise organic vegetables. I read the farm magazines and there's a growing need for heritage crops produced locally without insect sprays. Of course, if you did that, you'd need bees. They're everything when it comes to pollination."

"Daniel subscribed to *Modern Organic Farming*. We practiced it as much as possible. Easy there in Brazil, where chemicals and commercial fertilizers are too expensive to use. But jungle soil is thin. If you want to raise vegetables, either you move your gardens regularly, as the indigenous people do, or you find a way to enrich the earth. We buried fish guts and compost in our kitchen garden."

Her mood lightened as she remembered the joy of working with her plants in the early morning, loosening the soil around them and pulling the weeds. The village children had helped, making a game of plucking insects from her tomatoes, squash and peppers. Although she'd never been certain why they'd dropped each beetle, grub or ant into a tiny bark container and carried the insects away. Suspecting that the protein may have strengthened the family stew pot, she'd never had the nerve to ask.

"So you understand the idea," Thomas said eagerly. "Raising food without poisons. It's becoming popular with the Englishers, but you know our people. They like the high yields commercial fertilizer delivers. Once they get used to doing something in a particular way, they don't accept change easily."

"*Ya*, exactly," Leah agreed. "It was the same with the village elders. They were used to sending the young men out with nets to catch fish, but sometimes the river was so fast that it tore the nets, and sometimes there were few fish. Daniel and I built a fish

76

pond behind the clinic. We used the natural fertilizer that the fish provided to feed our garden and then drained the excess water back into the pond. We could catch fish for dinner whenever we pleased. At least when the predators or our neighbors didn't get them first." She laughed. "A fat fish in the missionary's pool is a temptation that's hard to resist."

"But you had a steady supply of food."

She nodded. "We were always trying to come up with small projects to improve the villagers' lives. We never did get them to stop drinking river water, but we managed to convince the elders to divert a stream upriver, filter it through charcoal and sand, and pipe it into the village. That way people weren't filling their cooking pots where the children bathed. They thought we were peculiar, but they humored us when they saw that fewer babies took sick and died in infancy."

"So you don't think my ideas are foolish?" Thomas asked.

"*Ne*," she protested, warming to the idea of a new project to put her mind to. "Not at all. Who would you sell to? I don't know how well organic produce would sell at Spence's market."

"I was thinking that maybe I could sell to

restaurants. Maybe specialty markets."

"That's a brilliant idea!" She smiled up at him. "I would imagine there's real money to be made if you could connect to the restaurants or the specialty markets in the cities. Daniel has a cousin — second cousin, really. Richard . . . Richard something. Hunziger, that's it. He lives near Lancaster. He and Daniel used to email back and forth. Richard grows organic fruits and vegetables and delivers them to restaurants in Philadelphia. He also makes a good profit on his laying hens. Even English people don't like store eggs once they've eaten ones from free-range chickens."

"Really? I'd love to have a chance to talk to him. But . . ." Thomas shrugged.

Leah thought for a moment. "Why don't you let me contact him for you? I don't have his address, but I'm certain that Daniel's aunt would. I'll ask Richard if he'd be willing to have you come out to Pennsylvania and see his operation. If you're interested?"

Thomas's features brightened. "Of course I'm interested. I could hire a driver and —"

"Why would you need a driver when I have a car and a license?" she asked. "It's not that far. We could easily go up and spend the afternoon. Actually seeing what he's doing would give you a better idea of what's involved. I know that growing organic vegetables and fruits is more expensive than regular, but Daniel said the profits were better, too. At least you'd be in a better place to make a decision, wouldn't you?"

"I would," Thomas said. A smile spread across his face and lit his intelligent, dark eyes. "You know, Leah, there's a lot more to you than people realize. You're not only pretty, but you're smart, and you're a good listener."

"Danki," she replied, thinking that perhaps there was more to Thomas than she'd thought, too. "But it's not such a big thing," she went on. "A trip to Lancaster would be fun, I think. And I would like to meet Richard's wife and family."

"So when can we go?" he asked eagerly.

"As soon as I can arrange it," she promised.

"And you have to let me pay for the gasoline and buy you lunch."

"I would like that," she assured him. "I'll warn you that I'm fond of hamburgers and fries. In Brazil I used to dream about crispy French fries from American fast-food restaurants."

"It's a date," he said as they turned into Sara's driveway. "And one that I can honestly say I'm looking forward to."

"Me, too," she agreed. And she had to admit that she was. Thomas might not be the man for her, but he was always fun to be with, and who wouldn't enjoy an unexpected holiday?

Chapter Five

Thomas lowered his window and gazed out at the rolling Pennsylvania farmland. The growing season was several weeks behind Seven Poplars, but it was full spring here all the same. The trees were bursting with new green leaves of every hue, and tractors and teams of workhorses plowed the wide fields. "A little rocky," Thomas pronounced, "but this looks like rich soil."

"Some of the best in the country, Daniel said," Leah replied. "The topsoil is deeper than a man's arm is long and the Pennsylvania Dutch are good stewards of the land."

"I think that some of my grandmother's people came from north of here. Some valley." He shifted in his seat to find more room for his legs. Leah's compact car was a tight fit for him. His head nearly brushed the roof, and even with the seat pushed back as far as it would go, he was cramped. Not that he cared about a little discomfort. He was enjoying the day, the new sights, and a break from the routine of everyday work. And they hadn't even reached Richard Hunziger's organic farm yet.

Leah signaled, slowed and turned off the wide road onto a narrower, hilly one. The houses on either side of the blacktop were a mixture of older stone residences and newer clapboard or brick. Young Amish children played in the yards, and women hung clothes on lines, swept porch steps and planted seedlings in large gardens. In one yard, a boy, no more than four years old, tugged at the halter of a fat brown-and-white pony. Pulling out of a driveway was an Amish man in an odd type of gray buggy, enclosed in the front as a normal buggy would be, but open in the back for carrying larger items.

"Amish pickup," Thomas said. "Pretty handy to have. I could use one of those for transporting lumber and building material."

Leah chuckled.

"What's so funny?"

"Not what you said. I'm sure a buggy like that would be useful. I was thinking about how far away this is from the Amazon. When the St. Joes didn't walk, they traveled by river in dugout canoes that barely rose above the waterline. Sometimes they'd load them down with entire families — fathers, the mothers, infants, kids and elders. I wondered why they didn't sink, but they never did."

"Mothers?"

Leah shrugged and grimaced. "Customs change slowly in the Amazonian jungle. It used to be common for the best hunters and the leaders of the St. Joes to have more than one wife at a time. Daniel and I did our best to discourage the practice, but . . ."

Thomas shook his head, amazed at what this young woman had seen and half wishing that it had been him traveling to faraway places and witnessing unfamiliar and outlandish customs. "Aren't there crocodiles in those rivers?"

"Some, but what we saw were a kind of alligator called a black caiman. Vicious beasts that grow to over sixteen feet long. The river also was home to poisonous snakes and flesh-eating piranha. Delicious, but very dangerous."

"You ate piranha?"

She laughed. "I'm sure we did. It wasn't considered polite to ask what your hostess put in her cook pot. Food, especially meat, is difficult to come by in the jungle. When the locals offer you food, you accept with thanks, ask a silent blessing that you won't die from it, and you eat it."

"So I wouldn't think you did much swimming in the river?"

She laughed again. "Hardly. The St. Joes swim naked."

Thomas felt his throat and face flush. Nudity was hardly a proper topic of conversation between a man and a woman, especially those who were dating. Not that this was a date. He'd come with her to learn more about organic-farming practices. As much as he enjoyed being with Leah — and she was always fun — she had a way of making him uneasy. She was so outspoken . . . so experienced. Not like other Amish girls he knew. He wondered if she'd ever be able to return to the quiet life in Seven Poplars or any other Old Order community after her life in the English world. Pity the man who did marry her. It wasn't natural, a woman knowing more than her husband.

"I don't think it's far now to Richard's farm," Leah said.

They passed an open courting buggy with a couple in it and several more gray family buggies before turning into a lane marked with a cheerful green-and-white sign that read Eden Hill Organic Fruits and Vegetables. A stone wall enclosed a pasture on one side with a flock of black-faced sheep. On the far side of the driveway were tidy rows of young apple trees.

A dog barked as the car pulled into the farmyard. The back door of a tidy white cottage opened and a middle-aged African American woman wearing a calf-length denim dress, a flowered apron and a head-scarf cap much like Leah's came out onto the steps. "You made it!" she called. "Richard! They're here!"

A husky redheaded man with a neatly trimmed beard followed her out onto the stoop. He came out to the car, followed by his wife, and shook hands with Thomas. "Did you have any trouble finding us?" Richard asked.

Leah shook her head. "*Ne.* Your directions were excellent."

"This is my wife Grace," Richard introduced. "The boys are in school, but you'll get to meet them later. They have a short day today for some reason."

"Teachers' conferences," Grace supplied.

Leah greeted Grace with a warm embrace.

"It's so good to see you. We've been worried about you," Grace told Leah. "We were so shocked by your loss. But you've been in our prayers every day."

Leah nodded. "I appreciate that. It means a lot."

"And I appreciate you taking the time to show me around your farm," Thomas told Richard.

Richard rolled up his shirtsleeves. "Glad to do it."

Grace chuckled. "Believe it. There is nothing Richard likes better than someone new to share his ideas with," she said.

"This is just a small place," Richard explained, leading the way across the yard. "Seventeen acres. And a lot of it is too steep to till for regular crops. But we're blessed with two springs that never go dry and some really fertile fields. By concentrating on growing only the best vegetables, I've been able to build up a steady demand for our crops, at top prices."

"And you think the market is there to make the extra expense of growing organic profitable?" Thomas asked. Leah and Grace fell in behind them.

"I do. It's hard work — I won't tell you otherwise — but I find it extremely rewarding, not just in financial reward but in knowing that I'm growing the healthiest food possible, food I want to feed my family. And I know I'm not polluting the ground or the water."

"That's one of the things that drew me to the idea of growing organic produce,"

Thomas said. "In many ways, it's the traditional way of farming, as our great-grandparents did."

Richard nodded enthusiastically. "You can start small, but land is the most expensive outlay. And you need something that hasn't been worked commercially. Otherwise, it will take a lot longer to meet the qualifications for organic crops."

"The acreage I have in mind has been in pasture for decades," Thomas explained. "It has good drainage and the soil's not too sandy."

"That sounds perfect. But finding your buyers is crucial. That's Grace's department around here. She carried free strawberries to a dozen of the best restaurants in Philadelphia and convinced the head chefs of two of them to give us a try. Since then, our farm has been in the black, and we've doubled and tripled our fancy-fruit sales. Farming has always been a hard way to make a living, but this has the greatest potential that I've seen, especially if you can find help to do the picking and packing."

"Which I think I can," Thomas said, thinking of the young Amish men and women in Seven Poplars who'd recently left school.

Richard led the way to the first of three greenhouses and pushed open the nearest door. "This is where I grow our salad greens and start seedlings," he explained. "With a combination of solar power and propane, I can keep the temperature high enough to grow tomatoes, lettuces and peppers, even in bitter weather."

Thomas stood back to let Richard's wife and Leah enter first. He noticed that Leah was carrying a clipboard and pen.

"To take notes," she said when she saw him looking at her. "You might like to know what varieties of cucumbers and squash grow best in a greenhouse, and what varieties Richard may have had problems with."

"I should have thought of that," he answered. Thomas was pleased that Leah showed so much interest in Richard's farming practices. For more than an hour they followed Richard up one aisle and down another, listening to him as they inspected the greenhouses and then went to see the field greens and strawberry patches.

"Blackberries and raspberries provide an excellent return," Richard said. "But they're labor intensive. They have to be picked, packed and delivered at the peak of ripeness. My customers love them, but the season is relatively short."

Duplicating what Richard Hunziger had done here would take years of work, Thomas mused, but the possibilities seemed endless. Finding markets for his products near Kent County, if he managed to grow them successfully, would be a problem. There were restaurants in Dover, but it was a much smaller city than Philadelphia, and Philadelphia was too far from Kent County to easily deliver fresh produce. But those were problems that could be worked out. What was important was that Richard was doing exactly what he'd dreamed of, and was doing it in a manner that supported his family.

Thomas and Leah had planned to be home early, but there was so much to learn from Richard and Grace and they were having such a good time that it had been impossible to refuse Grace's invitation to share a late lunch. And, after that, seeing that Richard had transplanting to do, it seemed only fair that he and Leah pitch in to help. They didn't leave the farm until almost supper time.

On the ride home, Thomas and Leah couldn't stop talking about all they'd seen. And he hadn't realized that he was hungry again until Leah pulled the little black car into a fast-food place. They purchased hamburgers, fries and lemonade from the drive-through window and ate it parked in the back row of the lot behind the restaurant. His double cheeseburger was so juicy that grease ran down his chin, and Leah had to mop it up with a napkin. They laughed over that and a dozen other silly incidents that had happened that day as they finished the last of the salty French fries and drained the last drops of lemonade.

"Not as good as Sara's," Leah pronounced.

"No, but it's cold and wet," Thomas replied. And then, chuckling and exchanging guilty looks like naughty children, they drove around to the drive-in window again and bought ice cream with chocolate and whipped cream on the top.

"Is it as good as you thought it would be when you were in the jungle?" he asked, indicating the ice cream.

She licked her spoon and grinned. "Absolutely."

All the way home they discussed all the possibilities of his starting his own organic-farm project that spring. Leah had good suggestions, and he was surprised by how much she had absorbed of what Richard had told them. "It's finding the markets that worries me most," he confided. "It won't be any good to grow organic vegetables if I can't find a place to sell them profitably."

"What if you tried the beach?" she asked

as they drove back onto the highway and turned south toward home. "Rehoboth and Lewes? I think there are lots of high-quality restaurants there, and I know they must have the customers who would want organic produce."

"But how do I deliver the fruits and vegetables?"

She thought on it for a moment. "Horse and buggy wouldn't work, would it?" she said.

"Hardly. It must be forty, fifty miles from my place to Rehoboth Beach."

She braked at a traffic light. "So maybe you need to go to Rehoboth and talk to some people at some restaurants. See if anyone's interested."

"I don't know who I would talk to. I can't just walk in the door. I'd probably have to have an appointment."

She glanced at him. "Actually, just walking in probably *would* be better. If you asked for an appointment, they could say they were busy. But if you walk in the door, a manager or a chef or maybe even an owner would probably talk to you just because you're Amish."

He frowned. "What do you mean *because I'm Amish*?"

"All day long they serve Englishers. Tourists in tiny bathing suits and short shorts and fancy clothes. How many Amish men come in? They'll be curious. You can take advantage of that curiosity. It's how Daniel and I met the more isolated tribes. We were a curiosity to them." She chuckled. "All we need is a few minutes of the restaurant manager's time. And if you could bring fresh organic vegetables to their back door, it would be a big help to their business, wouldn't it?"

He ran a hand through his hair. "What we haven't figured out is how I'd get those vegetables to them."

"One problem at a time," Leah said. "First we find you customers, then we'll worry about how to get the vegetables delivered."

Traffic began to back up. They came to a stop again, this time a long way from the light. Sirens wailed and an ambulance and several police cars passed. "I think there must be an accident ahead," Leah said. "I hope no one is hurt."

Thomas rolled down the window and strained his neck to see, but whatever had caused the trouble was too far ahead to make out.

On the left, a big sign flashed, advertising a bowling alley. "Oh," Leah said. "Bowling. I haven't been bowling in years. When I was little my *dat* used to take us. Do you bowl?"

"I've never been," he admitted. "Well, not since I was a teenager. And then, I was terrible."

"Me, too," she admitted.

They waited. More police cars passed. Not a vehicle in the lanes moved. There were cars in front of and behind them and a bumper-to-bumper line on the left. People began to get out of their automobiles.

"I think we may be here for a while," Leah said.

"It looks like it." He glanced at the flashing bowling ball and then back to Leah. "Maybe we should go bowling. It would be better than sitting here."

"Are you serious?" she asked.

He shrugged.

"Why not?" Leah exclaimed.

"And did you go bowling?" Leah's sister Rebecca asked as she reached for another of her mother's raisin sticky buns. They were seated at Sara's kitchen table with Ellie, enjoying a leisurely Saturday-morning visit. Rebecca's toddler, Jesse, was sprawled on the floor playing with a bag of wood alphabet blocks that Ellie had found in Sara's toy chest.

"Did they ever!" Ellie laughed. "Leah beat

him at bowling. Slaughtered him."

Rebecca chuckled. "I don't know if Sara would approve. It doesn't sound like very good behavior for a first date."

"It *wasn't* a date," Leah protested. She glanced from one to the other. "It wasn't! We went up to visit Richard and Grace so that Thomas could see Richard's farm and hear about his organic-vegetable business. It's something that Thomas is interested in. He doesn't want to be a blacksmith."

"Wait. Wait, let me get this straight," Rebecca teased. She was red-haired like Leah, like most of her sisters, and prone to sunburn. Since she'd been busy in her garden that week, she was sporting a crop of new golden freckles, sprinkled like cookie crumbs across her sweet face. "It wasn't a date. Yet the two of you, you and Thomas — the same Thomas who Sara wants to match you with — traveled out of state together, shared dinner with the Hunzigers, went to a restaurant, went bowling and didn't get home until after midnight? And you want us to believe that it wasn't a date?"

"It sounds like a date to me," Ellie agreed. "And a pretty racy date at that. Even for a Mennonite."

"It wasn't like that!" Leah declared. She knew that their kidding was good-natured, but it didn't stop her from flushing with embarrassment. "We went to get information about organic farming. We had to eat something on the way home."

Jesse's block tower tumbled and he began to fuss. Ellie got down on her knees to help soothe his distress. "Like this, Jesse," she said, and then handed another block to the chubby, ginger-haired boy. He was still young enough to wear a baby gown, the garment that all Amish children in the community wore until they were out of diapers. He had a full head of hair that Rebecca kept cut straight across his forehead that fell around his ears in auburn ringlets, and he had the cutest button of a nose.

Leah looked at her nephew with a lump in her throat. Strangely, it was becoming more and more difficult for her to remember her lost baby's features. She closed her eyes for just a few seconds and gathered her resolve. Her baby wasn't gone forever. They were just separated for a little while. She was here and, Lord willing, she would have other children to love. And they would all be together in heaven someday.

Rebecca nibbled on a piece of sticky bun. "If you want my advice, sister, I think you should give Thomas a chance. I think that's only fair to him. You *did* tell Sara you'd agree to get to know him."

Leah wiped the crumbs off her mouth with a worn linen napkin. "She didn't really give me — give *either* of us — a choice. This isn't all on me. Thomas wasn't thrilled with the idea, either."

Rebecca and Ellie exchanged looks.

"He *wasn't,*" Leah protested. "Thomas only agreed because his family is putting pressure on him to find a wife."

"Because I turned him down," Ellie put in.

"It's more complicated than that," Leah told Ellie. Then she turned to her sister. "You weren't there in Sara's office, Rebecca. You know how it all came about. Sara asked me to get to know Thomas and if it didn't work out, after six weeks, she agreed she'd find the kind of match I'm looking for. An older widower, someone settled in his life who needs a wife for his family."

Rebecca raised her Yoder blue eyes to meet Leah's gaze. "What you're talking about is a marriage of convenience," she said.

Leah got up and went to the stove on the pretense of warming her coffee with more from the pot. Of all her sisters, Rebecca had always understood her the best. Rebecca gave the impression of being easygoing, but she could go directly to the heart of a matter with unerring accuracy. "Is that so wrong?"

"Not wrong. We all know good marriages that have been arranged by family or friends, or even . . . a matchmaker," Rebecca said. "But your marriage to Daniel was very different. You fell in love. You went against your family and your church to marry him because you knew he was the one for you. You let your heart decide, not logic."

"I'm just . . . at another point in my life." Leah took care to choose the right words. She wasn't comfortable talking about this. About her feelings. Not with her sister. Not with anyone. She was still too raw from Daniel's and her baby's deaths. Too raw deep inside. "I don't want the same things that I did when I left Seven Poplars with Daniel." She threw her sister a pleading glance. "I wouldn't change my decision for the world, but I'm not certain that I would make the same one again." She inhaled, then sighed. "Let's say that I've come to value the quiet joys of life. I don't need excitement or romance. What I'm looking for in a husband is settled companionship, a partnership where each of us knows our place. No more jumping the traces for me. All I want is the peace of our community

97

and our faith."

"I think it's early days yet," Ellie advised. "Don't be so sure that God wants you to be the wife of a man old enough to be your father. There's much to be said for a young man with spring in his step. What if that young man God means for you is Thomas? There's more than a few men and women in Seven Poplars who say Sara plays a part in God's intentions when it comes to marriage. That she's His instrument."

Leah placed her cup on the edge of the counter, not sure how to respond. She had heard enough from her mother to know Sara's matchmaking skills were the best. That was why she'd come to Sara in the first place. But she saw nothing wrong with telling Sara what she wanted. Didn't everyone, man and woman, who came to her do that?

There was a sound of the back door opening and Leah let out a sigh of relief. "Need any help, Sara?" she called.

"Not a bit. Clothes are on the line." Sara entered the kitchen from the utility room, her cheeks rosy. "We have a visitor. Someone who's come to see you this morning, Leah."

"Who is it?" Leah asked.

"Your brother-in-law. Anna's Samuel. I asked him to come in, but he said maybe

98

you'd rather just come out to the buggy."

"Ach," Rebecca said. "I wonder what Samuel wants with you? I should be going, anyway. I've got a dozen things waiting for me at home, and Caleb and I want to ride over to look at a new driving horse this afternoon. It's a bit of a drive, so we told Amelia we'd pack a lunch and make a picnic of it."

"You sure you have to go so soon?" Leah frowned. It felt so good to be with her sisters again. She hadn't realized just how much she'd missed them until she returned to Seven Poplars. "I feel like you just got here. But you're not far away now."

"And we'll see plenty of each other," Rebecca assured her, retrieving her son.

Leah went to her sister and hugged her, then bent to give small Jesse a squeeze. He giggled and claimed whatever bit of her heart he hadn't earlier. "Come again soon," she urged Rebecca.

"And you come over to see me. The road runs both ways, you know." She kissed Leah's cheek. "And stop and talk with Caleb sometime. He's wiser than his years, sister. He may be able to give you spiritual comfort. You remember, he suffered a terrible loss, too."

"Maybe I will," Leah replied, thinking she

would do no such thing. Her grief for Daniel was private. She couldn't imagine what her sister's husband could tell her that she hadn't already heard from a dozen other well-meaning people.

Curious as to what Samuel wanted, Leah left Rebecca to say goodbye to Ellie and Sara and went out into the yard. He was standing by his horse's head feeding the animal bits of carrot and stroking the bay's neck and nose. The horse saw her coming and raised its head, nickering softly.

Samuel turned to her, his expression solemn. He was a kindly man, one that Leah knew made her sister happy. Samuel was a good father and a pillar of the church community, but being almost a generation older, she'd never known him well and had always held him in a kind of awe.

"Samuel. Good to see you," she called.

"I'm afraid I'm here as a deacon of the church rather than your brother-in-law," Samuel said. He was a big man, tall and wide of shoulder, with a full beard, streaked with gray.

Nervously, Leah thrust her hands into her apron pockets and waited.

Samuel took a deep breath. "I don't like doing this, and I hope you won't allow it to . . ." He broke off and started again. "You know as deacon, it is my duty to point out errors in the behavior of —"

"Behavior?" she asked. Now she was really curious. She'd barely been in Seven Poplars three weeks. "What have I done wrong?"

He grimaced. "Not wrong. Just unseemly. Bishop Atlee called on me early this morning and said that he'd had a disturbing report from someone in our community. You were seen returning at a late hour last night, in the company of a man."

Leah's eyes narrowed. "Aunt Martha reported Thomas and me to the bishop, didn't she?" She should have known that her interfering aunt would make a fuss. "There was no misbehavior, Samuel," she said. "Thomas and I went to Lancaster to visit cousins of my late husband and discuss organic gardening. Then we had something to eat, went bowling and drove home from Pennsylvania. Unfortunately, my car had a flat tire in front of Uncle Reuben and Aunt Martha's place. Uncle Reuben was in the barn delivering a calf, saw our flashlight and came down to the road to see what happened. He watched Thomas change the tire, and then I drove Thomas home and came back to Sara's."

"But you and Thomas *are* dating. And you were out all day and part of the night without a chaperone." He tugged on the brim of his straw hat. "I know you, Leah. I've known you since you were a child. You're a good girl. You wouldn't behave in a way that would shame your family. But Thomas has the reputation of being a bachelor who cuts a wide swath. It doesn't look good, Leah. Your aunt doesn't approve, Bishop Atlee doesn't approve and Anna and I are concerned for your reputation."

A knot twisted in the pit of Leah's stomach and she tamped down her rising ire. "I'm not baptized in the faith. I'm a grown woman, a widow. Surely, I can stay out after dark without my mother's approval."

Samuel shook his head. "That's part of the issue. You've been in the outside world for years. Now you've asked our bishop to return to the fold. It's important that you demonstrate that you can live by our rules. And you can't be accused of setting a bad example for younger women who look up to you."

She drew in a deep breath, resting her hands on her hips. She wasn't annoyed with Samuel; she understood that this was his responsibility. She just didn't like people telling her what to do. Not anyone. "So what does Bishop Atlee want me to do? I'm supposed to be getting to know Thomas.

That's what everyone wants. How am I supposed to get to know him if we don't spend time together?"

"It's not about you spending time with Thomas," Samuel responded patiently. "It's about the circumstances. You were unchaperoned."

"The bishop wants me to take my mother and stepfather with me next time Thomas and I go to Byler's for ice cream?"

Samuel frowned. "Anna said you wouldn't take this well. We mean only the best for you, Leah. We love you, and we want you to be accepted fully into the community. Bishop Atlee understands how difficult your position is. He asks that if you are out after dark, or if you and Thomas leave Seven Poplars in each other's company, you have a chaperone with you to prevent any uncharitable gossip. And it doesn't have to be your mother. Anyone will do." His expression hardened. "There is more at stake than your own situation. English people are quick to notice what we do. I know that you wouldn't want to cause our community to be a topic of criticism."

"Ne," she agreed reluctantly, crossing her arms over her chest. She was still annoyed, but she knew he had a point. "I wouldn't."

"Goot." Samuel's features softened. "Then

I'll tell the bishop that you understand and you've agreed to use a chaperone when necessary. *Ya?*"

Leah cut her eyes at him. Then she sighed and dropped her arms to her sides. "*Ya*, fine, I'll agree to it. I just won't agree to like it."

CHAPTER SIX

Midweek, Leah drove to the Stutzman farm in search of Thomas. While picking up groceries for Sara, she had run into a young Amish couple in Byler's Store who were friends of her sister Ruth. They had recently bought a small farm in Maryland, not far from Seven Poplars, and were raising organic asparagus and selling it commercially. They'd invited her and Thomas to visit, and she'd been impressed enough by what they had to say that she felt she needed to tell him about them.

The Stutzman place, consisting of two attractive houses, several barns and a handful of outbuildings, as well as the blacksmith shop, was set back off the road on two hundred and ten acres of high ground. Thomas's father kept a herd of dairy cows, which, along with the successful smithy, provided a comfortable living for the extended family.

Leah followed the gravel driveway from the road to the farmyard and parked her car near the blacksmith shop. A buggy stood near the open front doors. There was no horse between the shafts, but Leah could hear the ring of a hammer on steel and guessed that one of her neighbors was having an animal shod this morning. She was about to go in to search for Thomas when his grandmother came out of the house. "Morning," Leah called in *Deitsch.*

The older woman smiled as she recognized her. "Leah Yoder. I expect you're looking for our Thomas." Alma pointed. In the second field over, Leah saw a man turning up pastureland with a one-horse plow. "If you've a mind to save these old legs of mine, you can carry this iced tea out to him." She indicated a quart mason jar on a sideboard on the porch where she stood. "Plowing is warm work, and he's been at it all morning."

"I'd be glad to," Leah replied.

Two men came out of the smithy. One, Leah's sister's husband Roland, was leading a gray driving mare. The horse picked up her feet gingerly, obviously testing a new shoe. Roland nodded and smiled. "Morning."

She returned the greeting. She liked Roland. With him was Jakob, the new black-smith come to work for Thomas's grand-father. She'd met Jakob before so she wasn't surprised by his appearance. Jakob was a little person, like Ellie. And, like Ellie, despite his short height, he was an attractive and cheerful person. Leah was sure he'd be an asset to the community and she couldn't understand why Ellie seemed to have no interest in socializing with him. The man was a ginger, with thick, dark auburn hair. He had broad shoulders to balance his stocky build and his high forehead and large, cinnamon-brown eyes gave him an intelligent and pleasant appearance.

"Good day to you, Jakob," she called.

He smiled and raised a hand in a friendly way.

"A nice young man," Alma said, coming down the porch steps with the iced tea. "A help he'll be to my husband and son, I know. He comes as an apprentice, but there is little he needs to be taught. A good man with iron and gentle with the horses."

"I'm glad," Leah said. She put out her hands to take the jar of tea. "I'd best get this to Thomas before the ice melts."

"*Ya,* but best you take off your shoes before you walk out to them fields," Alma advised. "We had some rain last night and you'll get them good sneakers soaked through."

Nodding agreement, Leah removed her new navy blue cross-trainers and left them by the car before setting out to deliver Thomas's cold drink. As she walked into the first newly plowed field, she found herself chuckling aloud. The warm earth felt good on her bare feet, and the scent of fresh-turned soil made her almost heady with childhood memories. She'd gone barefoot in Seven Poplars much of the time, a pleasure that she couldn't allow herself in Brazil because of the poisonous snakes and fire ants.

She stopped and shaded her eyes with a hand, watching as Thomas reached the end of the field and turned back. What a beautiful picture he and the big bay Belgian made, almost like a painting on a calendar. They made a good team, the horse and the man, striding forward, muscles surging in unison as though they were one.

She'd always loved horses, especially the huge draft animals used for pulling wagons and doing the heavy fieldwork. She and her sisters had often taken turns riding on the horses when her father plowed or cultivated the crops. Sometimes, they'd run behind to pick up earthworms that were turned over by the plow. Later, after supper, her *dat* would take them all fishing. How she'd missed all this in the years she'd been away from Seven Poplars. And how she ached to have more children of her own that could grow up here and experience the wonderful life that she'd had.

"Please, God," she whispered. "Find someone for me who will make that possible." The glass canning jar felt icy cold between her fingers as she started slowly toward Thomas and the long dark cuts the plow had sliced through the thick sod of the pasture.

As she drew closer to the field that Thomas was working, she found that she couldn't take her gaze off him. Somehow, just watching Thomas and the sturdy draft horse made her smile. This was the life that she knew, simple and honest, and Thomas was the kind of man she understood best. If only he was older, more established, more mature. If only . . . But he wasn't, and that was that.

She had to be patient. Sara would find her a settled and respectable widower who needed a wife.

So why did watching Thomas Stutzman send a skittering sensation down her spine? And why was she walking faster, eager to reach him and tell him about her new friends? And why had she lain awake the night they'd gone to Lancaster thinking of what a good time she'd had? She pushed those thoughts away. Thomas was her friend. He was fun to be with, and that was all.

"Leah!" Thomas reined in the horse, and the plow jerked sideways and came to a halt. Thomas looped the lines around the handles of the plow, lowered it onto its side and came to meet her. "What's that? For me?" He grinned as he reached for the tea, removed the screw top and took a long drink. "Ah, good." He drank again, and she watched as beads of condensation dripped from the glass jar to run down his sweat-streaked neck.

He was dressed in everyday work clothing: denim trousers, lace-up leather work shoes and a short-sleeved blue shirt. The knees of his pants were patched, and his shirt was faded from long hours in the sun, but he didn't appear poor or shabby. With his tall, lean frame, narrow waist and broad shoulders, Thomas cut as sharp a figure as ever, she thought, and then chastised herself for doing so. *This is only a favor for Sara,* she reminded herself sternly. *Six weeks of being together, and she'll find a suitable match for me.*

Thomas drained half the jar of tea, wiped his mouth with the back of his hand and sighed. "You have no idea how thirsty I was." He placed the jar in the grass and removed his straw hat. His dark hair was as unruly as ever, thick and shaggy.

"You need a haircut," she said. "I could . . ." She broke off. She'd always cut Daniel's hair, and she'd almost offered to do the same for Thomas. She averted her gaze as she felt a warm flush creep up her throat and cheeks. Such familiarity wasn't accepted between unmarried couples. Had he been her brother or other close relative, or if he'd been a child, it would have been fine. "Could . . . mention it to your grandmother," she finished hastily in an attempt to cover her mistake.

"Ne." Thomas laughed. "I wouldn't let her near me with a pair of scissors. *Grossmama* never wears her glasses. The last time she cut my father's hair, he looked like a sheep that had just been clipped. On one side, she cut a good two inches shorter than the other."

Leah chuckled, grateful that he'd not pressed her on her near offer. But then he tilted his head and eyed her mischievously.

111

"Unless, you'd like to —"

"Not me," she protested, putting her hands up, palms out. "I'd do a far worse job of it."

He didn't reply. Instead, he retrieved the mason jar and finished the rest of the tea. "Thank you," he said when he had drained the last drop. "You saved my life."

"I doubt that."

"Absolutely." He grinned at her and she couldn't resist a smile. Thomas was being charming and he was hard to resist.

"What do you think of this as a spot to plant my garden?" he asked, encompassing the newly plowed field with a sweep of his hand. "The soil is rich, and since *Dat* put in the pond, the land is draining good."

"It's decent-looking soil, for certain."

He nodded. "I thought I'd start with tomatoes, peppers and greens."

"Where will you get your plants? It's a little late to start tomato seedlings, isn't it?"

"I found someone who will sell me organic seedlings that are a little more mature. I'm going to put in all heritage varieties: Brandywine, Old German, Nebraska Wedding, Cherokee Purple and Mortgage Lifter. I haven't found a source for organic plum tomatoes, but I will." He pushed back his hair and put his hat back on, pulling it down tight on his forehead. "You did me a tremendous favor when you took me up to Lancaster to meet Richard and his wife. I appreciate it."

She shrugged. "It's nothing. We had a good time."

"The best," he said. "Although it *did* get us in trouble with the bishop." Together they chuckled, and then he glanced back to where the horse stood patiently. "Actually, I was about to quit for dinner. *Mam* doesn't like us to keep her meal waiting. Would you like to eat with us?"

"*Ne,* I didn't want to interrupt your workday. It's just that I met someone at Byler's and . . ." She hurried to explain to him about the asparagus and the ready market for the crop. "I thought maybe you'd like to go and take a look," she suggested. "Of course, it takes years for asparagus roots to take hold, but once they do, it's easy to care for them and harvest."

"I'd like that," he said. "When can we go?"

"Anytime, I suppose. I've finished up my chores at Sara's." She hesitated. "Honestly, I'm going a little stir-crazy. I'm used to being busy from sunup until evening. It's strange not having my own home, my own work to be done."

He met her gaze and something in his told

her he understood. "How about this afternoon?"

"Aren't you going to finish plowing the field?"

Thomas shook his head. "*Dat* needs the horse to bring in a load of logs from the woods. If you'll stay for *Mam*'s fried chicken and dumplings, we can go right after dinner."

Then she remembered her conversation with Samuel. The same conversation, she learned, he'd had with Thomas first. "Are we supposed to have a chaperone?"

"Are we leaving Seven Poplars?" he teased.

She frowned. "But we'll be back early. It won't be dark." She pursed her lips. "Honestly, Thomas. I think the whole chaperone thing is a little over-the-top. Why should two grown adults need chaperones?"

"We follow church rules, Leah. I should have thought of it before Samuel had to speak to us. I blame myself. You've been away from it all, but I don't have that excuse. It's a small thing, a chaperone. And if you want to live Amish, you might as well get used to it."

"*Ya,* so I tell myself."

He smiled at her, his dark eyes warm and sparkling. "If you'll wait while I unhitch Dickie, we can walk back to the house together. I know my mother would be pleased to have you take bread with us. She and my grandmother always cook enough for twenty and then fuss about all the leftovers."

Leah wasn't entirely sure she should be sitting down to dinner with Thomas's family. If they were truly dating, with the intention of soon becoming engaged, that would be one thing, but this — what they were doing — she just didn't know if she felt comfortable joining the family. But she really did want to stay.

"Come on," Thomas urged. "You know you like chicken and dumplings. And there will be rhubarb pie. I cut the rhubarb yesterday."

"Fine." Leah chuckled. "You've convinced me." She followed him back to where he unhooked the singletree from the plow and carefully knotted the long reins and hung them over the Belgian's collar. Once Thomas had the horse under control, she approached and stroked his neck. "He's beautiful," she said. "I've missed horses. We didn't have any in Brazil. They don't thrive in the jungle."

Thomas spoke soothingly to the big horse and began to lead him back across the field toward the house. Leah hurried to keep up.

"I remember you riding your father's horses when you were a kid," he said. "You Yoder girls were something else."

"I loved to ride the draft horses," she admitted. "Their backs were so wide I wasn't afraid I'd fall off. Miriam showed me how to braid the horse's mane and pretend that it was the reins."

He stopped and looked at her. That mischievous smile slid over his face. "Would you like to ride now?"

"Now?" She knew her eyes got big. "But —"

Thomas cut off her protest by stepping close to Dick and cupping his hands for her to use to step up. "Dare you," he teased.

She glanced around. Who was there to see? Laughing, she caught a handful of Dick's thick mane, thrust her bare foot into Thomas's make-do stirrup and scrambled up onto the horse's back. Once she was up, she turned sideways and sat on him with both feet dangling and her skirt back over her knees, where it belonged.

He nodded approval, took hold of the gelding's halter and began to lead him once more.

"If we get in trouble for this, it's your fault," she declared, but she didn't care if it wasn't considered seemly for a woman to be riding a horse. Being up on Dick's back, feeling the familiar rhythm of the horse's gait beneath her, was exhilarating. "So if we need a chaperone this afternoon, where are we going to find one on such short notice?" she asked.

"Oh, don't worry, we'll find someone," Thomas promised. "My mother, my grandfather, maybe even both my grandparents. We'll have such a strict chaperone that even your aunt Martha won't have a word to say in criticism."

Leah chuckled as she remembered her aunt's disapproving face when she and Uncle Reuben had found them changing the tire in the dark. "Maybe we'd best play it safe and ask Aunt Martha herself," she joked.

"*Ne,*" Thomas protested. "Not her. I'd rather Bishop Atlee and both preachers, all crammed into the back of your car and fighting for a window seat."

The image of that in her mind made her laugh so hard that she had to tightly grip the horse's mane to keep from slipping off.

Several hours later, Thomas held open the car door so that his grandmother could get out. "Are you sure that double-dip cone didn't spoil your appetite for supper?" he teased. *Grossmama* had agreed to go with them to the asparagus farm, but Thomas had had to promise they would stop for ice cream on the way back. His grandmother loved ice cream. Strawberry. Always strawberry. Luckily, Byler's Store usually carried strawberry, and it was one of the places where you could still buy an old-fashioned ice-cream cone. Leah had chosen butter pecan, his personal favorite, a single dip, and he'd had two dips of rocky road.

Somehow, in the time that he'd gone into Byler's to purchase the ice cream, his grandmother had convinced Leah to return to the house to share supper with them. Thomas almost wished she'd refused. While his family had embraced her at the noon meal, he'd felt a little awkward. No one in his family knew that this wasn't a prelude to a real courtship. Leah had made that clear. He hadn't thought it was fair to get his family's hopes up, when in all likelihood, the dating would go nowhere.

The evening meal was a much simpler one: vegetable soup, buttermilk, crusty loaves of yeast bread and another helping of the delicious rhubarb pie. Jakob joined them as he did most evenings, and everyone had lots of questions about the visit to the Masts' asparagus fields. Thomas always enjoyed this time of evening with his family. Supper was a time for leisurely eating and talking. Sometimes they would sit at the table for more than an hour, and afterward his grandfather would read a short passage from the Bible before everyone scattered.

"I should be going once we clear up the kitchen," Leah said to his mother. "I'm afraid that I've imposed on your hospitality today."

"Ne," his mother answered, smiling. "We were glad to have you. Thomas never brings young women home with him."

"And if you hadn't come, Leah, I wouldn't have gotten ice cream," *Grossmama* reminded her. "You come every day, if you've a mind to it. I'm always free to go here or there."

Even Jakob seemed taken with her. "I like hearing about far-off places," he said as he settled down for a game of chess with *Grossdaddi.*

Leah offered to wash dishes, but his mother shooed her out of the kitchen. *"Ne, ne.* We can handle this. You and Thomas go sit on the porch and digest your meal."

"I really should be getting back," Leah protested. "Sara will wonder what happened to me."

His grandfather had shaken his head and

119

rubbed his generous belly. "No need to rush away. It will give you a bad stomach. Go and sit on the front porch with Thomas for a little while. And see if you can convince him to let his mother get that splinter out of his thumb."

"He has a splinter?" Leah asked.

"*Ya,* and first thing you know, it will turn bad, and he'll be swollen up to his elbow." Thomas's grandfather waggled his finger at him. "A fellow I knew one time, got a little splinter of wood in his foot and ended up with a wooden leg."

Thomas curled his fist, hiding the offending thumb with its dime-sized, puffy red infection. "It's nothing. The splinter will work its way out. They always do."

"Would you let me have a look at it?" Leah asked. "I won't touch it unless you want me to. But I've had a lot of experience removing thorns and splinters at our clinic. Once, I removed a rusty fishing hook that had gone through a child's hand. Your grandfather's right, you know. Splinters can cause a great deal of trouble if they aren't removed and the wound properly cared for."

Feeling trapped, Thomas looked from one to the other. "All right," he agreed reluctantly. "I'll let you look at it."

"*Goot,*" his grandmother said as she wiped

her hands on her flour-streaked apron. "I'll get the tweezers."

"And a needle," his mother added. "Just in case."

"Where do you want him?" *Grossmama* asked. "There may be more light by the window."

"I think we can go out on the porch," Leah suggested.

"Just Leah and me," Thomas said. His mother was handing Leah a spool of thread with a needle thrust through it.

"Tweezers might be better," his father suggested.

Thomas held open the back door for Leah. "We could sit on the step," he said. "Or the swing." This was ridiculous. He didn't need anyone to dig the splinter out of his thumb. He could do it himself. A little infection made it easier to slide out. He felt foolish and a little ashamed that such a small thing could make him uncomfortable. But he hated needles. He always had. Still, he couldn't look like a child in front of Leah. What would she think of him?

His mother tried to follow them through onto the porch, but he stood his ground and narrowed his eyes. *"Mam,"* he said softly. "I think Leah and I can manage one small splinter."

She rolled her eyes and laughed. "*Ya,* you young ones want to be alone. I should know that."

His father called, "Wife."

His mother handed him the tweezers. "Tell her that the needle is clean."

His *grossmama* came to the screen door with alcohol and Dr Ivan's All-Cure Liniment. It was the same liniment that they used on the livestock, more smell than antiseptic as far as Thomas was concerned, but it was easier to take it than argue. He pulled the wooden door firmly closed behind him and heard his mother and grandmother whispering. His father laughed, and Thomas joined Leah on the porch swing.

"Let me see," she ordered him.

Nervously, he extended his left hand. She took it between her smaller ones and turned it to examine the infected splinter. "It's nothing," he insisted.

"Let me be the judge of that," she said. "I'm the nurse." She glanced up and chuckled. "Well, not really a nurse, but close. And don't worry. I'm not going to poke you with a sewing needle."

Her fingers were warm. Gentle. He felt himself relax. They were probably right. He should have done something about the splinter before this. He couldn't afford to lose days due to an injury that didn't heal properly. Seeing the asparagus fields had made him even more eager to see what he could do with organic vegetables. And Leah's enthusiasm and suggestions added to his certainty that this was something possible.

"It must be sore," she said.

"Not bad." It was, but he wouldn't admit it. He glanced down. The red circle was growing, but the splinter was in deep. Getting it out wouldn't be pleasant. "What do you think?" he asked.

"Either we get it out or you go to the emergency room," she said. "This kind of infection can spread quickly. You can't afford to let it go any longer."

He nodded. "You're probably right. Do your worst."

"First, we soak it in warm water with salt in it. And then I'll see what's in the first-aid kit in my car. If your mother has ice, we can numb your thumb before we attempt to remove it. Sound like a plan?" She smiled at him.

An hour later they were still sitting side by side on the porch swing, and Leah was once again holding his hand. Between the soaking in warm water, the ice, Leah's soothing touch and her first-aid kit, they'd gotten the splinter out and cleaned up the inflammation. Except for a tiny pinch when the wood came out, it hadn't hurt. And the small discomfort was more than made up for by the gentleness with which she applied antibacterial ointment and carefully bandaged his thumb.

They'd talked easily about the day, about the rhubarb pie and about the possibility of asparagus and beets and cucumbers, and they'd laughed about his mother and grandmother's fussing over him. It had been a long time since he'd had such a good time with a young woman, and he'd never spent time with one that he'd been willing to be so open with. He didn't want the evening to end.

Shadows began to fall across the porch and still they laughed and talked as if they did this every day. Thomas found himself studying her: her eyes, her freckled nose and her lips. What would Leah do, he wondered, if he tried to kiss her? He'd kissed Violet and Mary and Jane, to name a few girls. It had been fun and he'd liked it very much. But, suddenly, he wanted to take Leah into his arms and not just kiss her, but hold her. And he got the feeling she felt the same way.

He leaned closer. For an instant their gazes locked. He looked deep into her clear blue eyes and she began to lean toward him.

And then the moment was gone.

She pulled back and got up. "It's getting late. It's been a wonderful day, but it's time I went back to Sara's."

He jumped up. Had he misread her? He was usually good at knowing when a girl wanted to be kissed. And he was pretty sure he hadn't been mistaken. Not the way she'd looked at him. "Leah."

"Thank your mother for dinner and for supper," she said. "And your grandmother for going with us today, to act as chaperone." She moved away from the swing.

"Leah," he repeated. "I . . ."

"Good night, Thomas." She hurried down the steps and across the yard to her car.

He stood there watching her go, wishing she wouldn't, wondering if what he thought was happening between them really was.

CHAPTER SEVEN

Leah shifted her weight on the wooden stepladder and rubbed hard at the schoolhouse windowpane with her cleaning cloth. On the other side of the glass, Ellie wiped away ammonia spray as she continued her amusing story. One of her first-graders had found a frog on his way to school that morning, had put it in his lunchbox and forgotten about it until he opened the box. The frog had leaped out onto the head of one of the Miller girls and continued on hopping from desk to desk, causing an uproar among the students.

Leah laughed along with Ellie. How she wished she'd been here to see the turmoil caused by one small frog. It was four thirty in the afternoon on Friday. The children had gone home for the day, and Leah had come to help Ellie wash the schoolhouse windows. It was odd being back at the school where she'd spent so many happy years as a child. Ellie's stories reminded her so much of similar events when she was a girl, but she couldn't believe how much smaller the building seemed now. For years her mother had been the teacher at the Seven Poplars school, and her sisters and many of her cousins had been here with her. Good days, she mused, carefree days.

Other than the addition of the back porch and a closed-in area for coats, boots and lunch boxes, not much had changed since she'd been a student here. The scarred hardwood floors, the plain white vertical wainscoting and the smell of chalk and Old English furniture polish hadn't changed. The school consisted of a single room with an old-fashioned blackboard, rows of tall windows, and a potbellied stove that stood in the center and provided heat and a place to warm hot chocolate or soup on cold winter days.

"It was sweet of you to volunteer to help," Ellie said from the other side of the glass. Her friend's high voice pulled Leah out of the past and back to the present. "The school year ends next week and I want the building to look its best for parents' night," Ellie said.

"Glad to help." Leah finished the last pane and descended the ladder. The adjoining window was the last on this side of the schoolhouse, and she wanted to complete this section before Thomas arrived to pick her up. "More hands make every task easier."

Ellie pushed open the window and reached out to take hold of the top of the stepladder to steady it as Leah moved it into place. Practical Ellie had her sleeves rolled up and wore an oversize apron over her bright blue dress. She'd removed her *kapp* and tied a navy scarf over her neatly braided and pinned blond hair. As usual, Ellie was a delight to spend time with. Leah liked the woman more every day because when you were with her it was impossible to be gloomy. No wonder the students adored her. Ellie's love of life was infectious.

"Where is Thomas taking you today?" Ellie asked.

"Nowhere in particular. Just for a drive." Leah continued washing the windowpanes, taking care not to miss any spots. "I mentioned how much I missed traveling at the speed of a horse and buggy the last few years. And he offered to quit work early today and take me for a drive. He borrowed an open courting buggy so we wouldn't need a chaperone."

Ellie's heart-shaped face lit up with mischief as she pushed up the window. "I guess that depends on where your ride takes you."

Leah gave her a questioning look.

"If he goes by Tyler's Woods Road, he might just stop to water his horse at the pond. You remember how young people like to go there. It's off the road. Pretty with all the trees coming out in bud this time of year. But I warn you, if you agree to go there with him, don't be surprised if Thomas tries to steal a few kisses."

"Why would you say that?"

Ellie laughed. "Because he tried it with me." She shrugged. "It didn't work, but he made the attempt."

Leah shook her head. "It's not like that with us."

Ellie stifled another sound of amusement. "*Ne,* of course not."

"Really," Leah protested. "He's fun to be with, but —"

Ellie leaned on the windowsill and gave her a disbelieving look through the open window. "You like Thomas and you know you do. Admit it."

Leah resisted the urge to toss her dirty sponge at her friend. "I do like him, but not in that way. Thomas and I are friends. I'm helping him find out more about organic farming. He thinks that's what he wants to do, and I think it's an excellent idea."

"So is Thomas thinking about how he'll provide for a wife and children?"

"Eventually." Leah chuckled. "But even if he is, it doesn't mean . . ." She didn't finish the sentence. The other night on the porch at his house, Thomas had come very close to kissing her. She hadn't let him, of course. She'd ended the evening before she had to tell him she didn't want him to kiss her. Or maybe she'd ended the evening so quickly because she was afraid she might have let him kiss her.

Ellie giggled. "*Ne,* of course he's not thinking of you. Just because you're courting."

"We're not —" Leah cut herself off. She wasn't going to have this conversation with Ellie again. Instead, she said, "I'm sure Thomas will make a fine husband for someone. He's just not what I'm looking for."

"Or me." Ellie dropped her cleaning rag into a bucket. "But he isn't hard on the eyes, you'll have to admit that."

"Looks aren't everything," Leah said. "I want an older husband, someone settled. I've had excitement in my life." She unconsciously lowered her voice. "Now, I just want a peaceful life, a new baby to hold in my arms, someone to walk to worship with, a husband who will take care of us and make the decisions."

Ellie's blue eyes clouded with concern. "Are you certain that's what you want, Leah? I haven't known you all that long, but I know Hannah and your sisters. You don't seem like the kind of woman who wants her husband to think for her."

Leah didn't answer. Instead, she climbed down the ladder, emptied her bucket of dirty water and joined Ellie inside the schoolhouse.

Ellie came to meet her and took Leah's hands in her small ones. "I'm sorry," she said. "I need to learn to hold my tongue. I shouldn't have pressed you about your private business. You know better than me what will make you happy."

"*Ne,* it's all right," Leah insisted. She could feel the emotion gathering in her chest. In another moment, she'd be bawling like a baby. "I do think that's what I need, but . . ." She shrugged and forced a smile. "The truth is, sometimes I don't know what I want. Thomas is wonderful but he's so . . . so . . . lighthearted."

"He just plays the part of the cutup because that's the sort of person everyone expects him to be. He's really quite sweet."

"But he wasn't right for you."

"No, he wasn't," Ellie agreed. She released Leah's hands and perched on one of the first-grader's desks, her sneakered feet dangling over the edge. "I want to marry someday. I want a family. Children. But I've never met a man that suited me. And . . ." She gestured around the schoolroom. "I really love teaching the children. I can't imagine giving this up."

"Because you haven't met the right man." Leah felt relief that the conversation had moved on from her personal life to Ellie's. "You know, I had supper with Thomas and his family the other night, and Jakob asked about you. He seems intrigued."

"Don't tell me that."

"Why not?" Leah asked. "Jakob's single. And he is a very attractive man."

"For a little person, you mean?"

"Don't put words in my mouth. That wasn't what I was thinking." Leah folded her arms. "What I was thinking was that Jakob Schwartz may be short, but he's still a hottie."

"Leah!" Ellie's eyes widened in surprise and then together the two of them burst into giggles.

"Well, he is," Leah said when she could talk again. "And he's nice. I like him. You should give him a chance."

132

"Absolutely not," Ellie said with a shake of her head.

"What? You don't like him because he's little?"

"I don't want anything to do with him because everyone — including your mother — is trying to shove us together. Just because we're both little people. From the first time he came to Seven Poplars for a visit, Jakob this and Jakob that is all I've heard. And now that he's living here, it will only be worse. I'm not picking a husband because of his height." Ellie slid down off the desk, pulled her cleaning rag from a bucket and began washing the blackboard. "No more talk of Jakob. Agreed?"

"Agreed," Leah said. "But only for now, because —"

"Look!" Ellie pointed out the window. "Here comes your Thomas. And he's driving that fancy sorrel horse of his."

Leah glanced out the window and she couldn't help the quiver of anticipation that ran through her. "It's a beautiful horse, isn't it?"

"Beautiful and fast . . . like his master," Ellie teased.

Leah reached up to make certain that her *kapp* was in place and then untied the big work apron and hung it on one of the iron

133

hooks along the back wall.

"Take a sweater," Ellie advised. "Unless you are depending on Thomas to keep you warm."

"Stop," Leah protested. "I am *not* sweet on Thomas. There will be no hugging and certainly no kissing."

"*Ne,* of course not," Ellie replied. "Because you're not sweet on him." Her laughter echoed in Leah's ears as she hurried out of the schoolhouse and walked across the grass toward Thomas.

"Can't you get Irwin to weed this for you?" Leah asked her mother. Irwin was a boy her mother had taken in years ago, and was a member of the family now. She'd stopped by for morning coffee and found Hannah in the garden cleaning up her strawberry patch. The berries weren't fully in bloom yet, but they soon would be. Here and there a white blossom peeked through the lush green leaves.

"Irwin has a part-time job with the Kings helping build lawn furniture. He's there today. Besides, I like getting out in my own garden," Hannah replied as she stooped to yank out an offending sprig of dandelions from under the edge of a strawberry plant. "These are Pocahontas," she explained.

"They ripen later than the Surecrop, but they're sweeter. They make the best strawberry shortcake."

Leah dropped to her knees on the opposite side of the row from her mother. In Brazil, she'd sometimes worn a light blouse and a split skirt, with knee-length trousers under it, for working in her garden. Since they had visitors only rarely and the St. Joes wore next to nothing in the hottest season, she hadn't felt that she was too immodest. But she'd given away the skirt and the pants when she'd said goodbye to her jungle home. The Old Amish residents of Seven Poplars would never understand or accept such laxity in dress in one of their members. Fortunately, she'd worn her oldest dress today, and either the garden dirt would wash out or it wouldn't.

Her mother raised her head and smiled at her. "It's good to have you home, Leah. You'll never know how much we missed you."

"I missed you all, too," she replied as she dug out the root of a stubborn chickweed. "Every day." She'd left Seven Poplars for a different life, and she'd done her best to serve God and to be the wife that Daniel deserved. If he hadn't died, she would be there now, working beside him. But coming home, being with her family, walking the fields and woods that she had while growing up had gone a long way to healing the unbearable pain of losing Daniel and her child.

"I prayed for you to come back to us." Her mother's gaze was full of compassion. "I just didn't expect it to be this way."

"Me, neither," Leah replied. She and Hannah had so much in common — both had been widowed far too young. What she didn't know was if she possessed the strength her mother had. "I just hope I'm making the right decision in asking Sara to find me a husband."

Hannah looked up. "Have you prayed on it?"

"*Ya.* And I feel in my heart that this is what I should do. That it was right to become Mennonite, and now it's right for me to join all of you and become Amish again."

"And you have no doubts about taking on the responsibility of our faith?" her mother pressed.

Leah smiled. "None at all. I'm looking forward to it. I know it's where I belong."

"It eases my mind to hear you say it." Hannah went back to weeding. "Now you need to stop worrying and let Sara do her job. It will all come out right. You'll see."

"I hope so."

From the side yard, Leah heard her sister Susanna's laughter as she and her husband David tossed a ball back and forth. It was a large plastic ball, nearly the size of a basketball and bright orange, but neither of them could manage to catch it on the first try. Instead, they giggled and squealed and chased the rolling ball across the grass. Susanna's *kapp* hung askew, her face was smudged with dirt and her hands and dress were grubby, but she was clearly having a wonderful time. Susanna, like Ellie, had the gift of enjoying every moment of life.

When Ruth had written that their mother had given her permission for Susanna to marry David King, Leah had been surprised. Growing up, Leah had always thought Susanna the light of their home, one of God's special people. But she'd never expected Susanna to wed. She was childlike in so many ways. Now, seeing how happy Susanna was, and getting to know David, who'd also been born with Down syndrome, Leah was beginning to understand her mother's decision.

"Thomas is working this morning," Leah explained to Hannah, "but he'll be off by one. We were thinking of going to Rehoboth this afternoon to talk to some of the managers of local restaurants about possible markets for Thomas's organic vegetables."

Hannah dropped a handful of weeds into a pile and looked up with a serious expression. "Would you like me to come along as your chaperone?"

"*Ne, Mam.* I would not," Leah replied firmly. "I thought that —"

Hannah laughed, and Leah broke off in midstatement. Realizing that she'd been had, she began to chuckle as well.

"How about Irwin?" her mother teased.

Leah shook her head. "Absolutely not."

"You have to have someone. You can't go to Rehoboth for the day without a chaperone."

"Actually, I thought maybe that Susanna would like to ride down with us," Leah said. "I could take her to see the ocean and buy her cotton candy. You know how she loves to ride in the car."

"I do. Maybe more than is good for her. But you're right — she would enjoy it." Hannah got up and dusted the dirt off her skirt. "I'll tell her to wash up and change into her church dress and bonnet."

"I can do it." Leah glanced down at her own dress, streaked now with garden soil and grass stains. "I need to freshen up

138

myself. I have another dress in the car. I'll go and change before Thomas gets here."

"You watch your sister close," her mother warned. "You know how she is. And I wouldn't want her to come to harm out among the English."

"I'll take good care of her," Leah promised. "And I'll have Thomas to help me."

"And that's supposed to make me feel easier, with his reputation for mischief?"

"I think that was when he was younger," Leah said. "He's been very responsible around me."

Hannah looked skeptical. "I hope he appreciates your help. And you. He couldn't find a finer wife anywhere."

Leah rolled her eyes. "*Mam,* I told you before. I don't see this working out. I'm just giving it the six weeks because that's what Sara and Thomas and I agreed to."

Her mother studied the strawberry bed with its spreading rows and straw-laden aisles. "Better," she pronounced. "Much better. Martha always thinks her strawberry bed is the best one in the county. Wait until she tastes my Pocahantases and Raritans."

"If I didn't know you better, I'd think you were a little prideful," Leah teased.

"Maybe a little," her mother admitted. "It's a fault I own to. And the good Lord knows I have more than a few to repent of."

"You're not alone." Leah smiled and hugged her. "I've missed you more than I can ever say."

Hannah's lips were warm on her cheek. "Go and have fun. Just don't let Susanna out of your sight."

As she'd suspected, Susanna was delighted by the prospect of a holiday. Her round face glowed with excitement as she bounced from one foot to the other. "Cottoned candy! I like cottoned candy. Blue."

"We'll see if they have blue," Leah agreed as she urged her into the house. "But we have to hurry. Thomas will be here soon, and we have to be dressed and ready."

"Ready!" Susanna agreed. "Ready for cottoned candy."

Twenty minutes later, Thomas came striding up her mother's lane. Leah and Susanna were on the porch waiting. "We're all set," Leah said, getting eagerly to her feet. She was almost as excited as Susanna was — she was just better at hiding it. "Susanna's coming with us. She was thrilled when I asked her to be our chaperone."

"Goot, goot," Thomas replied with an easy grin. "I'll talk with a few of the restaurant managers and then we can take a stroll on the boardwalk. I'll buy my girl some Thrash-

er's French fries. Best anywhere."

"Thomas's girl." Susanna clapped both hands over her mouth and giggled.

Leah let his comment pass without correcting him. The three of them were nearly to the car when her mother came across the yard. "Wait," she said. Smiling, she took Susanna's hands and looked into her face. "You do what Leah says, and stay with her. Do you understand?" Squeezing Susanna's hands tenderly, she kissed her on the cheek.

Susanna nodded vigorously. "Leah said . . . said blue candy. Cottoned candy."

"Try not to get it in your hair," Hannah advised. She straightened Susanna's bonnet and tied her *kapp* strings under her chin.

"She'll be fine, *Mam*," Leah assured her.

Her mother's gaze turned to her, running up from her black leather shoes to her black tights and calf-length Lincoln-green skirt, topped by a white blouse and black cardigan. Leah's cheeks grew warm as her mother inspected the lacy white scarf that she'd tied over her hair in place of her usual conservative Mennonite prayer *kapp*. "If you're to be one of us, you'll have to give up fancy clothing," she advised gently.

"I will, *Mam*. But I don't have to just yet."

Hannah sniffed, reached behind Leah's head, untied the scarf and retied it beneath

141

her chin as she had Susanna's. "So the ocean wind won't blow it off," she said.

Leah looked from her mother to Thomas. He grinned and shrugged.

"I might know you'd take her side," Leah said. She brushed her mother's cheek with a kiss and took Susanna's hand. "Time to go."

Thomas climbed into the front seat. Leah fastened Susanna's seat belt in the back and then slid into the driver's seat. She was just about to start the car when David trotted toward the vehicle, waving his arms.

"Me!" he cried. "Me, too. Going!"

"Wait for King David!" Susanna cried. "Come on, King David."

Leah tried not to smile. David was dressed in his Sunday black coat and trousers, and wore a fast-food paper crown on his head. Leah looked at Thomas. "We can't say no." The backseat was small, barely large enough for two small passengers. And David was definitely not a small person, but there was no way she could leave him behind.

Thomas said, "Get in, David. We'll make room for you. And be sure to fasten your seat belt."

Susanna squealed with pleasure and clapped.

"*Ya,*" David agreed as he squeezed into

142

the back. "Make room."

Leah looked out the window to where her mother was standing by the gate.

"Naturally, your sister is bringing her husband along. They're inseparable." Hannah waved. "You young people have fun!"

Leah glanced over at Thomas. He shrugged, and they laughed together. "We will," Leah called to her mother as they drove out of the lane.

But when she reached the end of the drive, she stopped the car long enough to untie her scarf and retie it as it had been when she'd come out of the house. She waited for Thomas to comment, but when he wisely held his peace, she said, "Now you know why I'm staying with Sara."

Thomas laughed, and Susanna and David giggled. As they drove south toward the ocean resorts, Thomas turned on the radio and found a Christian station. When a familiar hymn that was popular at the social gatherings began, he started to sing along with it. Susanna and David, both loud and off-key, joined in enthusiastically.

We're going to have fun today, Leah thought. She knew that she should admonish Thomas for the forbidden radio, but she didn't have the heart. And by the time they reached Dover and turned onto Route 1,

she'd shed her doubts and was singing along
with the rest of them.

CHAPTER EIGHT

"What did he say?" Leah asked as Thomas came out of Breeze, a popular new eatery on Rehoboth Avenue. It was the last restaurant on his list for the day and she was eager to hear how it had gone.

Thomas smiled and nodded. "I think it went all right." He glanced to the wooden bench on the sidewalk where David and Susanna were enjoying their cotton candy. "Those two good?"

Leah looked over her shoulder. Her sister and brother-in-law were safely where she'd left them, heads together, talking, so she turned back to Thomas. "They're great. Enjoying their cotton candy. Don't keep me in suspense. What did they say? Were they interested in buying your produce?"

He took her hand, guiding her away from the door. "A definite maybe," he said in *Deitsch.* He switched to English. "The manager listened to what I had to say."

"So a firm maybe?" she asked. They'd had two definite nos, restaurants that had other sources they were happy with, one yes and another maybe.

Leah had enjoyed seeing how much Thomas's confidence had increased with each restaurant he walked into. Dealing with Englishers wasn't always easy for the Amish and she understood his nervousness. But today everyone Thomas had approached had been kind, and they hadn't treated him as if he were some quaint oddity or a nuisance.

He nodded. "A definite maybe. They'd like me to stop back when I have salad greens and berries to show them. Breeze is known for healthy food, but I wouldn't have to have the certified organic vegetables. They wanted to know how many days a week I could deliver produce." His expression was serious, but Leah could read the excitement in his eyes.

She smiled up at him, making no effort to free her hand. Vaguely, she was aware of passersby studying them with interest, but she ignored them. It was natural that they look. How often did you see such a good-looking Amish man in his best black coat, hat and trousers in the midst of a sea of tourists in flowered shorts, bright-colored

146

T-shirts and oversize sunglasses? "What did you say?"

"I told him I could deliver every two or three days, depending on what was in season and how much they were willing to take. And I made it clear there would be no Sunday deliveries." Thomas grimaced. "The big question is *how* I'm going to deliver."

"You're resourceful," she answered. "I'm sure that if you can find reliable customers, you can find a way to get your produce here. Maybe you can hire a driver with a van or something."

He smiled down at her. "*I'm* resourceful? If it wasn't for you, I wouldn't have gone to see Richard's farm or the asparagus fields. And I know I never would have thought to come directly to restaurants to find a market. You're an amazing woman, Leah." He grinned. "Not just a pretty one."

She felt herself flush with pleasure. Thomas was a flirt, and he probably said things like that to girls all the time, but she was glad she'd taken the trouble to wear something nice today. She shouldn't have cared so much what he thought, but for some reason, she did.

Confused and conscious of her quickening heartbeat, she pulled her hand from his and stepped away, putting distance between

them. Thomas knew that it was unaccept-
able for the Amish to display affection in
public. Even married couples were expected
to refrain from holding hands or hugging,
let alone kissing, as she'd seen an English
girl and boy doing on the street just a few
minutes ago. She put a hand to the back of
her head, checking her scarf. "We need to
get back to Susanna and David," she said,
to cover her loss of composure.

"They're fine." Thomas gazed intently at
her, as if he was seeing her for the first time.

Leah's heart fluttered again. It had been
so long since she'd felt this way about
someone. Too long.

When she realized the direction her
thoughts were going, she reined them in.
Thomas, she told herself, *this is just Thomas.
We're friends, nothing more. He isn't the man
I'd want to spend the rest of my life with.* But
she found herself unable to break eye
contact with his warm brown eyes. She
couldn't tear her gaze away. He took a step
closer and, against her will, she felt giddy.
The honk of cars, the voices, the clatter and
hum of the busy street faded, as if in the
midst of all this activity, they were the only
ones on the busy sidewalk.

"Leah?" Thomas took her hand again.

She felt a tingling sensation that started at

her hand where he touched her and drifted upward. She tried to say something, but her mind went blank. Her lips formed his name, but no sound came out.

"Leah, I . . ." He leaned toward her and she had the strongest suspicion he was going to try to kiss her.

And if she didn't break this intimacy immediately, she was afraid she would let him this time.

"Leah —"

"We . . . we should go. You — you don't know Susanna," she blurted as she hastily backed away. "When she wants to, she can move as quick as a cat's paw. You can't imagine what mischief she can find to get in to." The outer wall of the restaurant loomed behind her, keeping her from retreating any farther. "One time she snuck out in the middle of the night, hitched up the pony and cart and drove off to be with David." Leah knew she was babbling foolishly, but it didn't matter. *She had wanted him to kiss her.* She still wanted him to. She had to get control of her emotions before it was too late.

"They look innocent enough to me." He took another step toward her.

Leah glanced at her sister. Susanna was still sitting on the bench, black stockinged legs crossed at the ankle and bonnet seated snuggly on her head. Apparently, she and David had finished every bite of their blue cotton candy and were well into their tub of Fisher's caramel popcorn.

"I'm not sure what's happening here between us, Leah," Thomas murmured, searching her gaze, "But I think we should . . . talk about it."

She shook her head, unable to break eye contact with him.

When he spoke again, it was a whisper. A whisper meant only for her. "What is it you want, Leah?"

"French fries!" The words just came out of her mouth. She blinked. "*Ya*, Thrasher's French fries. You promised you'd buy us fries." She could feel her cheeks flaming.

Thomas broke into a grin and took a step back. But Leah felt like she hadn't fooled him. He knew what she'd been thinking. He knew she wanted to be kissed as much as he wanted to kiss her.

"I did, didn't I?" He gestured toward the ocean, a few blocks away. "Let's go. I'll get you fries. And pizza, if you want it. Whatever you want, I'm your man."

Once they'd purchased boardwalk fries, Thomas looked around for a bench where they could sit and enjoy them in the warm afternoon sun. There were a lot of people on the boardwalk: couples and families strolled down the noisy walkway amid the blaring music from the children's rides and the calls of hawkers urging passersby to play their games, as well as the bustle of the many fast-food stalls. Seagulls added to the clamor with their squawks and diving forays to snatch fallen bits of pizza, popcorn and corn dogs.

David and Susanna walked just ahead of him and Leah, hand in hand. The boardwalk was too crowded for them to walk four abreast, and guiding David and Susanna was a little like herding cats. Distracted by the colorful sights and smells, both of them were apt to dart away in opposite directions without warning. Ten paces down the boardwalk, Thomas realized why Leah wanted to find a place to sit as quickly as possible.

Thomas spied a bench just being vacated by a family and was about to direct them that way when Susanna stopped short in her tracks.

"Ooh!" she cried. "King David! Look!" She pointed toward a booth boasting a wall of plush stuffed skunks with huge silky tails and enormous bows around their necks.

David slowly began to smile. He turned

and walked toward the stall, followed by Susanna. Leah tried to hold her back, but there was no stopping her once she got something in her head.

"Susanna!" Leah hurried to catch up with her.

David came to a halt in front of the counter. He pushed his black-framed glasses up on his nose and studied the game. Thomas came up behind David and scanned the interior of the stall. Oversize white soda bottles formed a square, and stacks of colored hoops waited on pegs just out of reach. Strings of colored lights blinked on and off to the blare of music. The purpose of the game was to successfully toss the hoops over the necks of the bottles. It appeared simple, but Thomas knew better.

"Step right up! Try your luck! Win a prize for the little lady!" the attendant called.

"No," Thomas said. "He doesn't want —"

But David had already pulled a ten-dollar bill out of his pocket and handed it to the fortysomething sunburned man wearing a Dolle's Taffy T-shirt and a straw cowboy hat. The man slid David's money into the pocket of his canvas apron, but Thomas gave him a stern look. "Five dollars only," he said. "Give him change from his ten."

The man frowned. "It's three throws for a fiver."

Thomas stepped closer to the booth. "Change," he said firmly.

With a shrug, the man did as he asked.

Susanna giggled and hopped from one foot to the other excitedly. "I want that one," she said, pointing at the nearest stuffed skunk. "Please." Susanna's speech was difficult to understand, but it was clear to Thomas what she wanted.

"Ya," David said, stroking his neatly clipped beard. "For Susanna."

Thomas looked helplessly at Leah. She shrugged. Games of chance on the boardwalk probably weren't what Hannah had in mind when she'd allowed Susanna and David to come with them to Rehoboth, but David clearly knew his own mind. His Down syndrome condition might be clear to anyone who looked at him, but after spending time with him, Thomas understood that, although speech was difficult for him, David was less challenged than Susanna in many ways. And the money was David's. He had a right to try to win a skunk for his wife if he wanted to. Interfering might be worse than letting him lose his five dollars. Thomas glanced back at the attendant and nodded. Leah took David's

153

frozen lemonade.

"Win a prize with every hoop!" the man called out.

Several teenagers had stopped to watch. "You can do it!" one of them called.

"Yeah, go for it," another chimed in.

David's grin faded as he took the first hoop from the man. Susanna patted his arm and stood on tiptoe to whisper something to him. He pulled back his arm and threw the rope ring. It bounced off the lip of one bottle, seemed ready to settle onto another and then slid between them. David groaned.

Susanna put out her hands for the stuffed animal.

"Ne," Leah explained. "David has to get the ring on the bottle."

" 'Nother one," David said in *Deitsch.*

More fun seekers had stopped to watch. David suddenly had a cheering section of sunburned Englishers. Thomas was so glad that Leah had been able to convince David to leave his paper crown on the backseat of the car and wear his straw hat.

"Throw it easy," urged one of the kids.

There was a general moan as David's second attempt missed the bottles altogether. Susanna clapped. David looked at her and a smile spread over his round face. The man handed David his final ring. The onlookers grew quiet. Thomas wondered if God would forgive him if he prayed that David would make this one. David tossed the ring. Again, it struck the lip of a bottle, bounced and spun. But this time, the hoop flipped and settled solidly over the neck of the end bottle in the row.

"Winner!" the man cried. "We have a winner here!"

One of the teenagers slapped David on the back. "Way to go, bro!"

The crowd clapped as the attendant unhooked the stuffed animal skunk Susanna was pointing at and handed it to her. She clutched it and stared at David with shining eyes.

Thomas made eye contact with Leah. She was wiping away tears and smiling, too. "Thank you," she murmured.

"Don't thank me," he said. "David made the winning throw. He won the prize."

David beamed and threw back his shoulders.

"Try for a second one?" the huckster asked.

"Ne," Thomas said as he ushered his charges away. "One skunk is plenty."

David took Susanna's hand in his and they walked together down the boardwalk until Leah spied two empty benches. She settled

Susanna, David and the stuffed skunk onto the first one facing the boardwalk and then glanced at Thomas expectantly.

Thomas flipped the back of the other bench so that they could sit the opposite way, with a view of the ocean. Leah slid onto the bench and looked out at the waves. Thomas sat next to her. Neither of them spoke, but after a while he took her hand in his. He knew he was taking a chance, but he couldn't help himself.

He saw her cheeks color, but she didn't try to free her hand.

He sighed, content. The breeze off the ocean, the sun on his face and the smell of caramel popcorn and salt water . . . It was a glorious day. He couldn't remember ever having such a good time.

"No kissing!" Susanna hollered suddenly in English. "No kissing, sister!" This time, to Thomas's dismay, her words came out so clearly that a woman pushing a baby carriage heard her and laughed.

"Shh." Leah raised a finger to her lips. "Church voice, Susanna."

"No kissing!" her sister repeated just as loudly, falling into *Deitsch*. "King David and me can kiss. *Mam* says 'married kissing.' 'Door-closed kissing.' But you can't kiss Thomas. You have to marry Thomas. Then

156

kissing."

"Thomas and I aren't kissing," Leah answered quietly, in *Deitsch*.

"Holding hands. I see you," Susanna waved a chubby finger. "You like Thomas. But no kissing."

"All right, no kissing," Leah agreed. Chuckling, she looked at Thomas. "You heard our chaperone."

Thomas gave her hand a squeeze. He was so happy he felt as if he'd burst with joy. *I really am falling in love,* he thought. *Even Susanna can see it. I'm falling in love with Leah Yoder.*

Carrying a willow egg basket, Leah climbed barefoot over the stile that led from Sara's pasture to her aunt and uncle's farm. It was a gorgeous May morning, and the fields and woods were tinted a dozen shades of green. It had rained the previous night, and the grass glinted with water droplets like so many diamonds. Her mother's strawberries were ripe and promised a bumper crop. Hannah had invited her to come and pick some, and the back lane that ran through her mother's orchard was the quickest way to get there. Leah wanted to pick several quarts and would surprise Sara with a strawberry shortcake.

As she crossed the lot where Sara's mules were corralled and then the meadow, Leah let her thoughts stray. She'd dreamed of Daniel last night. Not a bad dream or a sad one, but she'd awakened feeling that there were things that had to be said between them.

After their baby had died of the fever, Daniel had lingered, his temperature soaring to dangerous highs and then receding, giving them hope that he would survive it. They'd had time to talk, time to say their farewells and time for Daniel to tell her that she must be strong.

She paused on the far side of the stile, her feet cushioned on the thick moss, a chorus of birdsong around her, and let Sara's basket slip to the ground. She remembered every word that Daniel had said to her that last night. He hadn't been afraid of death. He'd been secure in his faith. Daniel had been the strong one, and she'd clung to him, begging him not to leave her alone.

"But God is with you," he'd whispered, his voice low and urgent. "Never forget that, Leah. God has a plan for you. All you have to do is let Him take control. Follow where He leads you." She'd wept, telling him that she didn't want to live without him, that life held nothing without him and their baby.

But he'd refused to accept that. "I know you," he'd rasped. "You Yoder girls are as solid as granite. You won't crumple when storms batter you. Find a good man and marry again. Have more children. You have to promise me that you will."

"I can't," she'd answered, but Daniel had insisted. How could she refuse him anything at that moment? And so she had agreed.

And now, finally, after more than a year, she could see that he'd been right and she'd been wrong. She only wished she could tell him.

Leah looked around. On a branch overhead, a wren scolded her, and, higher up, she caught sight of a squirrel. But there were no humans around, not a single person to hear her and think she'd taken leave of her mind.

She closed her eyes. She didn't know if Daniel could hear her up in heaven, but she liked the idea that maybe he could. She certainly felt as if he'd been watching over her since he'd been gone.

"Daniel?"

She concentrated, trying to picture Daniel in her mind. She could summon a fuzzy memory, but nothing sharp or definite. "Daniel, if you can hear me, I want you to know that I'm all right. I'm doing what you said. I didn't think I would ever laugh again or take pleasure in a hot cup of tea or the soft feel of a new-hatched chick. But I do. It hasn't been easy. You know me. I hate to give up control. But I'm trying to just let go, to be a leaf in the wind, to see where God takes me. And it's good, Daniel, really good."

She opened her eyes. The love she felt for Daniel and her baby was still there. It would always be there. But so was God's love. His mercy had set her free to live again . . . to seek a second chance at being a wife and a mother. She wondered if she should tell Daniel that.

But then she guessed he already knew.

A smile spread over Leah's face as she picked up the basket, her heart feeling lighter. She had gone a hundred yards when she was startled by the crash of underbrush and a frantic bellowing. She looked up to see a brown-and-white cow come charging out of the woods straight at her.

"Stop her!" shrieked a woman. "Don't let her get away!"

Leah jumped aside and the cow thundered past, a rope trailing behind her. The animal skidded on the path, pitched forward, scrambled up and continued on at an awkward lope into a huge open field.

Out of the trees came a disheveled and red-faced woman brandishing a broom. "You let her escape!" she shouted at Leah. "She ran right by you."

"Nearly ran me down," Leah agreed, trying not to smile.

Aunt Martha's once-white apron was muddy, and her faded lavender dress had a three-cornered tear in the skirt. One sleeve had come unstitched at the shoulder seam and hung down, exposing six inches of her upper arm. A blue scarf and tangled lengths of gray-streaked hair dangled down her back, and a twig with three leaves sprouted from the crown of her head. She wore men's rubber muck boots that came to her knees, probably not her own as they were several sizes too large. Worse, the boots were caked with something that smelled suspiciously of barnyard fertilizer, some of which had stained the hem of her dress.

"What are you staring at?" Breathing hard from the chase, Aunt Martha dropped the broom, scrunched her hair into a messy bun and tied the scarf firmly over it. "Why didn't you catch her?" The twig with the three leaves still protruded from under the scarf.

"Sorry," Leah mumbled, trying hard not to laugh.

"Worthless heifer." Her aunt wiped her

muddy hands on her skirt. "I told your uncle that she was nothing but trouble. She'd be more use if we sent her to Gideon's butcher shop for hamburger." She stopped her tirade, caught her breath and advanced on Leah. "Where are you off to? Your mother's, I suppose. I'm sure you weren't planning on stopping to spend time with me."

"*Mam*'s expecting me," Leah explained, still trying to control her impulse to giggle. She'd noticed a chicken feather clinging to her aunt's scarf. A tall, thin scarecrow of a figure with sharp features and a narrow, pinched mouth, Aunt Martha could never be truthfully called more than a plain woman. This morning, however, she looked as though someone had put her in a burlap bag full of garden dirt and shaken her.

"Has ideas on her mind, that one," Aunt Martha said.

"Excuse me?" Her aunt couldn't be talking about Hannah, could she?

"The heifer." Aunt Martha's lips firmed into a thin line and her voice dropped to a whisper. "Those beef cattle of Samuel's. He has a new bull. And that one . . ." She gestured in the direction the cow had gone. "Sweet sassafras, Leah, you were a married

162

woman. I shouldn't have to spell it out for you."

"Oh," Leah replied. "Your heifer is running after Samuel's —"

"What did I just say? Some things shouldn't have to be said straight out, should they? But then your mother always did let you girls run wild. When you married that Mennonite boy and went off to God knows where, I said to her, 'Hannah, now you see what comes of it.' Thank the Lord you've seen the error of your ways and come home to the faith. But had she listened to me, you'd have married your own kind to begin with."

Leah didn't know where to begin answering that and so she didn't say anything.

Aunt Martha didn't seem to notice. "And speaking of marriage, you need to remember what's expected of one of our girls. I saw you and that Thomas walking home just about dusk the other night. Right down this path. I wouldn't have noticed if you didn't cut through my farm. I mind my own business, you know. Anyone can tell you that." Her aunt gave her a probing look. "Seeing a lot of him, aren't you?"

"I am, but . . ." Leah drew in a breath and prepared to defend herself. "But we were chaperoned. Anna's son Peter was with us."

"Saw the two of you. Didn't see him."

"But he was with us. Bishop Atlee said we needed a chaperone after dark or to travel out of Seven Poplars, and we've done as he asked."

Martha nodded. "So you should. A widow or not, a young woman has to guard her reputation, and that Thomas, he's always been a wild one."

"Sara arranged the match," Leah said. "She thinks —"

"Oh, I know what she thinks. And this time, I have to agree with her. You know Thomas's name was mentioned for my Dorcas. Everyone said, 'Thomas is going to come into a bit of land and he has a trade.' But my Reuben and I, we thought she could do better. We told her to wait. The right man would come along." She picked up her broom. "That heifer will be long gone by now. Reuben will have to send the hired boy to fetch her home."

"Well, it was good to talk with you, Aunt Martha." Leah shuffled her feet. "Sorry about your cow."

"You go on, pick your strawberries. Ours haven't come on yet. I expected your mother to invite me to come over and pick, but she hasn't. Too many of her own to feed, I suppose, to think of a sister-in-law." She sniffed. "But you mind what I said, Leah. Listen to the bishop and don't do anything that could cause rumors of misbehavior between you and Thomas." She smiled. "Come to think of it, I may have been the one to put a bee in Sara's bonnet about the two of you. 'That Thomas might be perfect for Hannah's Leah,' I told her. 'Both of them being a little odd.' And Sara took my advice and matched you up. I told Reuben that you were walking out together as soon as I heard. And he said, 'You're right, Martha.' " Martha walked away, talking to herself now. "I'm right so often about who should be courting whom, maybe *I* should become a matchmaker."

CHAPTER NINE

When Leah arrived back at Sara's after driving her sister and nephews to the dentist, she didn't expect to find Thomas there and busy at work. He was digging a hole in the side yard using a Bobcat, a small specialized tractor with a backhoe on the rear. Thomas saw her and waved before shutting off the engine. "You're out early," he called to her.

"Dental checkups for Johanna's older boys. No cavities."

She got out of the car and crossed the lawn to the edge of the excavation.

"They keep you busy, driving to doctors and such," he said. "Your sisters."

"Not just my sisters. Friends, family, half the people in Seven Poplars, I think," Leah replied, tickled to see Thomas, even though she wasn't expecting him. "I won't be allowed to keep the car once I join the church, but until then, I'm glad to help out the community. Saves them paying a driver. *Gross-*

mama needs to go to the lab for some blood work soon. I promised Anna I'd take her."

She was also driving Ruth to the midwife for a checkup, but that wasn't information she intended to share with Thomas. Her sister was in the family way, something women liked to keep private until their condition became obvious. "What are you doing? Don't tell me Sara is putting in a swimming pool?"

Thomas chuckled. "Close enough. She wants a fishpond with a fountain. It's going to be solar powered."

"I didn't know you could drive one of those things." She pointed at the Bobcat. How handsome he looked, she thought. Just the sight of him on this bright June morning made her want to clap for joy.

"There's a lot about me you don't know," he replied with a grin.

Typical Thomas, always ready with a smart answer. She looked at the hole in the lawn and then back at the machine. "I meant, I didn't know that the elders approved of tractors. Shouldn't you be digging this with a shovel?"

He shook his head. "It would take a *lot* of shoveling. The community voted to allow heavy machinery on a limited basis." He chuckled. "So I'm fine as long as I don't use it as transportation. I just can't drive it home."

She laughed. "How did you get it here?"

"The equipment-rental place delivers." He climbed down off the tractor seat and pointed to the excavation. "Sara asked me if I wanted to put in a bid for the pond, a screened-in gazebo and an arbor. She wants a welcoming place where her couples can sit and talk privately while remaining in full view."

"It will be lovely, but she didn't say a word about it," Leah said.

"That's Sara. She likes to have all her ducks in a row before she talks about her plans. This shouldn't take too long, and it will give me extra money to put into my garden. Speaking of which . . ." He pointed at her. "Would you like to come over after work and see my peppers and tomato plants?"

"I would." The two of them spent three or four evenings a week together and she never grew bored with being with him. Sometimes they just went for a walk or fishing in the pond, but often they made themselves busy planting seedlings or even weeding his small but growing garden. "Any idea when the first tomatoes will be ripe enough to sell?"

He considered. "Let's see. This is the first

of June. So far, we've had excellent weather for growing. If we get enough rain, I should be picking cherry tomatoes by early July. Four or five weeks. God willing."

"*Ya*, God willing," she repeated. They had much to be thankful for. So far, Thomas's plans for raising and selling his organic vegetables had gone smoothly. He was excited about it, and she was as well. It was good to have a new project to help bring to fruition. "Is it too late to put in more spinach? *Mam* has had luck with a heritage variety that stands the heat better. And those baby eggplants. Maybe there'd be a market for those."

"Leah, are you keeping Thomas from getting my fishpond dug?" Sara came from the house carrying glasses of iced tea.

"We were talking about Thomas's garden," Leah explained. "His heritage tomatoes are growing well."

Sara chuckled. "You were talking, all right. I shouted out the window to see if you'd like something cold to drink, and you were so intent on your conversation that you never heard me."

"Sorry," Leah said. She smiled, feeling a little bit as if she'd been caught doing something naughty. But it was Sara's idea that they see each other, so she refused to feel guilty about it.

"I'm just teasing you." Sara handed each of them a glass of tea. "I've been wanting to catch the two of you together. Do you realize that your six weeks is up?"

"What?" Thomas nearly choked on his tea. He started to cough, and when he'd cleared his throat he shook his head. "It can't be. Six weeks?"

Leah thought for a minute. Could six weeks really have gone by so quickly? But when she did the math, she realized Sara was right. It *had* been six weeks since she and Thomas had agreed to see each other. Almost seven weeks. She gave a little laugh. "She's right. The time has flown, hasn't it?"

Sara planted her hands on her ample hips. "So?" The question was directed at Leah.

"So . . . what?" Leah repeated.

"So, what do you think?" Sara pointed at Thomas. Then she gave a wave in his direction. "No need to ask you. I already know you've fallen head over teacup for our Leah." She returned her attention to Leah.

Leah took a breath. She hadn't contemplated what she would say because she hadn't thought she'd ever be in this position. But facts were facts and she wasn't afraid to admit she'd been wrong. "You were right, Sara. Thomas and I are a good match." She went on, matter-of-fact. "I didn't think so when you first brought up the idea. In fact, I was *sure* that he wasn't what I wanted." She gave him a warm look. "Nothing against you, Thomas. I just thought . . . Well, never mind what I thought. What matters is that I was wrong. We're compatible." She shrugged. "So I guess we should move forward."

Sara narrowed her gaze. "So, you two have talked about this?"

"Not . . . exactly," Leah went on. "But, you're fine with this, right, Thomas?" She glanced his way.

He nodded rapidly, looking a little surprised.

It was just like a man to be surprised by something so apparent as this. She and Thomas were compatible — they had the same values, the same desire to live in a way that was pleasing to God. And they both needed spouses. It was really that simple. Leah looked at Sara again. "Thomas and I are both seeing Bishop Atlee for baptismal classes. We're happy with each other, so I don't see any reason why we shouldn't begin official courting. We could probably be married in autumn, once both of us have been baptized."

"You seem to have your mind made up,"

Sara said, looking directly at Leah. But then her gaze drifted to Thomas. "I see no reason you can't court, but I'm not sure you're ready to set a wedding date."

Leah looked down at the watch locket that she wore on a chain around her neck. "Oh, look at the time! I've got to pick up Anna and *Grossmama.* I hate to run, but I promised I'd be at Anna's early. It's not so easy getting *Grossmama* dressed and into the car. Her health really seems to be failing in the last few months."

"Will you be home for supper?" Sara asked.

"*Ne,* don't wait on me." She turned to go, then back to wave. "See you later at your place, Thomas. Have fun with the Bobcat."

Thomas drank the last of his iced tea and watched Leah drive out of the yard in her car. Vaguely, he was aware that the tea was icy cold, just the way he liked it. The tea quenched his thirst and the June sun was warm on his face. Still, he felt a little odd, even out of sorts. Had he just heard what he thought he'd heard? That Leah didn't just want to marry him? That she wanted to set a date for their wedding? It was what he'd wanted, what he'd prayed for. So why, now that it was going to happen, was he not

172

bursting with excitement?

"You look confused," Sara said.

"Shocked, I think," he admitted. "Leah and I have been really enjoying each other's company and getting to know each other. I'd hoped she'd want to move forward. I *think* she has feelings for me and I definitely . . ." He felt his cheeks grow warm. He'd never been shy about talking about a girl before but maybe because he'd never felt this way before. "It's just . . . I . . ." He stopped and started again. "I guess I didn't realize that we . . . that Leah was ready to take the next step."

"But you are, too, aren't you?" Sara's gaze was direct and a little uncomfortable. "You're ready to move toward marriage?"

He nodded. Honestly, he was a little bewildered by Leah's casual declaration. He had just assumed that at some point he and Leah would talk about the original arrangement they'd made with each other and how it had changed. When they'd agreed to see each other seven weeks ago in Sara's office, he'd thought he'd been buying himself some time with his grandfather. And Leah had agreed to date him to please Sara with the understanding that if it didn't work, the matchmaker would find her an older widower. Neither had thought they'd end up discussing marriage. What had he missed?

Of course, he'd never seriously dated anyone like this before. Maybe it wasn't something you were supposed to talk about to each other. "I'm in love with Leah," Thomas said quietly. "So that means that we should be courting. And marrying in the church."

"Is she in love with you?"

He dropped his gaze to his boots.

Sara made a sound in her throat. "You've not discussed your feelings for each other or the idea of marriage." It was a statement, not a question. "You would feel easier if the two of you had talked it out before Leah said something to me?"

He squinted, thinking. "Should we have? I mean, is that what couples do?" He shrugged. "This is all new to me. I've never seen my mother and father talk about personal stuff."

"But you wouldn't hear private conversations between your parents, would you?" Sara said. "Matters that are private between a couple are not for others to hear, not even a dear son."

Thomas scratched his head. "So . . . are you saying Leah and I *should* have talked about this? Alone?"

Sara pursed her lips. "It seems to me that

if you and Leah intend to marry and spend the rest of your lives together, that decision should be made together."

"So . . . we should talk about it?" he said. "We need to?"

"I think you two need to get in the habit of talking things through. Not just thinking the other knows what's going on in your head."

He nodded, thinking, staring at the toe of his boot. "Leah's not a big one for talking about how she feels. She's more one for just doing. But I have my own faults. And I want Leah for my wife." He looked up at Sara. "I want her any way I can get her. And that's the truth."

Sara smiled. "You must be cautious, Thomas. Marriage is for the rest of your lives. Once joined, you are together until death. You might feel differently in ten years, even twenty. And it isn't fair to change the rules then. You need to establish things now, before you make that commitment."

He continued to look at her, not certain where this conversation was leading. "Establish them how?"

"There is nothing wrong with telling Leah that you want to talk things out before she makes decisions for both of you. Even when you agree with what she thinks, it's important that you both have your say."

He nodded. "I'll think about it, Sara. I will."

"Be certain you do. These things need to be worked out between you before you exchange vows. There's nothing that says you have to marry this fall. Not if you're not ready. Marry in haste. Repent in leisure."

"But . . ." He handed her his iced-tea glass. "I don't understand, Sara. You're the one who said we were right for each other. This match is your idea. Now are you saying it's not?"

"That's not what I'm saying, Thomas. But I've been doing this for a long time. Every couple has issues to work out. And they are best worked out *before* marriage. That way there are no unpleasant surprises for either of you later."

"I don't see any problems between us."

"I'm glad of that. But you need to take this one step at a time. You're not a raw boy. You're used to doing things a certain way, which is natural. And Leah has been through a lot. You're not marrying a twenty-year-old girl."

"I know that." He hesitated. "About your fee. Do I pay it after the wedding or —"

"No need to worry about it. Hannah and

176

Albert are taking care of Leah's portion, and your grandfather has already come to an agreement with me."

"So you think that fall would be too soon for us to marry?"

Sara shook her head. "No, I didn't say that, either. Plenty of time to set a date for a November wedding. What's important is that you each marry with a free heart, that you find what you want in the union."

"I want to make a home with Leah, to have children if God sends them, to serve Him and our community."

Sara smiled. "I can't think of better reasons to marry." She patted his arm. "You're a good man, Thomas, and Leah is fortunate to find someone like you."

"And me, her." He grinned at Sara. "But I'd better get back to work on this pond. They charge rent by the hour, and we're talking on your pocketbook, when I should be digging."

"I'll leave you to it, then." Sara took the glasses and went back to the house.

Thomas let out a sigh of relief. He couldn't wait to get home this afternoon and tell his family that he and Leah intended to set a date for their wedding. That should please them — especially his grandfather. It pleased him well enough.

He climbed back into the seat of the Bobcat and started the engine. Maybe there was something to what Sara had said about telling Leah they needed to talk things out between them. But, right now, he was happy that she'd agreed to be his wife.

Two days later, Leah, Thomas and Ellie were driving back from Rehoboth on Route 1 in Leah's car. Thomas had delivered assorted orders of lettuce, spinach and strawberries to three restaurants, and Ellie had come with them as chaperone. They'd all enjoyed a walk on the beach after the vegetables had been delivered, and both Ellie and Leah had gotten slightly sunburned.

"Next time, we'll remember to put on sunscreen," Leah said as she glanced into the mirror to see her sunburned nose. Her sister Miriam tanned, but she never did.

"I offered to lend you my hat," Thomas teased. He tapped the edge of the wide straw brim. He had the hat in his lap because he was tall and the car had a low roof. Ellie, in the backseat, had plenty of room.

"Wouldn't that be a sight for the Englishers?" Ellie said chuckling. "But it wouldn't be right for you to go without your head covered, Thomas. You would have to wear

178

one of our *kapps.*"

Leah and Thomas both laughed at the thought. Traffic was light, and Leah was enjoying the drive. The whole day had been fun. She always enjoyed being with Ellie, and having her along was easy, without any awkwardness. Nothing fazed Ellie, not the noise and clamor of the boardwalk or the open stares of the tourists and their children.

"Does it ever bother you, Ellie?" Leah asked. "Having people point at you in public?"

"Because I'm short or because I'm Amish?"

Leah laughed. Her friend had a good point. And she liked the fact that they didn't have to avoid the subject of her stature. "Because you're short."

"When I was little, it frightened me that people were always staring," Ellie admitted, "but then I decided it was because I was pretty, not because I was little."

Leah grinned, glancing at her in the rearview mirror. "Only you would say such a thing."

"*Ya,* but it's true, isn't it? I'm short, but I'm cute. And God gave me a brain. I have my health and my eyes and two hands and two legs. Why should I feel sorry for myself because I'm not taller? If I —"

"Did you see who that was?" Thomas said, interrupting Ellie. "Walking along the highway?"

"Ne," Leah answered. "I was concentrating on that pickup. He's switched lanes multiple times and I was just trying to stay out of his way."

"Where's the next turnoff?" Thomas asked, looking over his shoulder. "We have to go back."

"Go back? Why?" Ellie asked. "Who was walking along the road?"

Thomas pointed to a traffic light ahead. "There," he said. "Make a U-turn. I think that was Jakob."

"Jakob? You mean Jakob Schwartz?" Leah asked. She put on her signal, moved over and guided the car into the turn lane. "What do you suppose he was doing walking?"

"He was going fishing today on a boat out of Bowers Beach. A driver picked him up before daylight this morning. I'm sure it was Jakob," Thomas insisted.

Ellie groaned. "It's not like little people are as common as cows around here."

Leah looked in the mirror as she made her turn and saw the sour expression on Ellie's face. "You wouldn't want us to leave him by the side of the road, would you?"

she asked.

"*Ya,* I would. Unless you plan on putting him in the trunk. If anyone in Seven Poplars sees me in the backseat of this car with him, my life is over."

Leah accelerated in the southbound lane. "Why will your life be over, Ellie? I've met Jakob. He's a very pleasant person. Smart. And funny. You two should —"

"*Ne,* we shouldn't. Your grandmother asked me after church when we were crying the banns, me and the little man. And your aunt Martha said out loud during one of the hymns that us both being little didn't mean our children would be short. We could have normal children."

"But that isn't Jakob's fault," Thomas defended.

Ellie sniffed. "If you'd heard as many hints and suggestions and offers to have us both to dinner as I've heard since that man first came visiting to our community, you'd understand. When I marry, *if* I marry, it won't be because my husband has to be a little person. And as for our children being normal, I think I *am* normal," she fumed. "It's the rest of you who are too tall."

Leah spotted Jakob, made the next U-turn and pulled to the shoulder of the road behind Jakob, who continued walking. She

181

put on her flashers. Pulling off like this made her nervous. Seeing Jakob walking the busy highway made her even more nervous.

Thomas got out and shouted. "Jakob! It's Thomas!"

The little man turned, grinned and waved, and trudged back to the car. In one hand, he carried a saltwater fishing pole and reel, in the other, a tackle box. "Glad to see you, I am, Thomas."

"Get in," Thomas told him.

Jakob leaned in the open passenger window. "I didn't think to be picked up by a friend. Leah." He nodded a greeting, then glanced into the backseat, saw Ellie and did a double take. "Ellie Fisher." His smile spread until his whole face crinkled with good humor. "God is truly good to me."

"The tackle box will go in the trunk," Thomas said, taking it from him. "Fishing pole, too, if I break it down." He made his way to the back of the car as Leah released the trunk latch. "You can jump in the back."

"Or ride in the trunk with the tackle box," Ellie muttered.

Leah stifled a chuckle. "Be nice," she warned, turning to look into the backseat.

Ellie grimaced. "Maybe Thomas would like to ride back here with him."

"Thomas barely fits back there." Leah

made a face. "He's too tall."

"We could fold *him* in half," Ellie suggested.

"Fold who in half?" Thomas asked, closing the trunk. "Hop in, Jakob."

Ellie slid over and Jakob got into the backseat with her.

"Sorry if I smell like a fishing boat," he said. "I'm afraid I will stink up your car."

Ellie drew herself up stiffly and moved over closer to the door, leaving a space between them. *"Ya,"* she agreed. "You do smell like a fishing boat."

"What happened?" Thomas asked, getting back into the front seat. "Why are you walking? What about the driver who picked you up?"

"The bay was rough. The driver got seasick," Jakob explained. "So seasick somebody else had to drive him home. They offered to take me, but he lives way south of Dover, so I decided the best thing to do was start walking."

"It's a long way from here to Seven Poplars." Leah checked her rearview mirror and eased back onto the road. "At least twenty miles, maybe more. You should have called the chair shop or another driver."

"Don't know any others," he said. "It never occurred to me that the Englisher who drove me to the dock wouldn't take me home. And I don't have the number of the chair shop." He shrugged. "I don't have a cell phone. And I've walked farther than this before. I might not have got back to the farm until after dark, but I would have gotten there."

"I'm glad we came along when we did," Thomas said. "Did no one else offer you a ride?"

"Two Englishers," Jakob said, "but they'd carried a cooler of beer onto the boat. I don't hold with alcohol, and I'll not ride with anyone who's been drinking."

"Did you catch any fish?" Thomas asked.

Jakob shook his head sadly. "Nothing I could bring home. And I had my heart set on fried fish."

"I like fish, too," Leah said, changing lanes to get around a tractor trailer hauling chickens. "Saltwater fish are my favorite. Especially flounder or trout."

"How about you, Ellie?" Jakob asked. "Do you like fish?"

"Can't abide them. Not the smell, not the taste."

"I'm sorry for that," Jakob replied. "You don't know what you're missing."

"I think I do," Ellie said.

Leah glanced at Ellie in the rearview mirror. She was staring straight ahead, her hands fisted at her sides. Her cheeks were pink and her mouth set in a thin line. Leah was surprised. She'd never seen Ellie so out of sorts, and it was unfair to blame Jakob, who'd done nothing but have a bad day. Leah hoped he wouldn't notice her friend's rudeness.

"Tell you what," Thomas said. "Let's stop in Wyoming. There's a family restaurant there that serves good food at fair prices. I'll treat you all to supper. And Jakob, they always have fish on the menu. You can enjoy your fish supper after all."

"That's a great idea," Leah said. "Ellie?"

"Lovely," Ellie said in a tone that clearly said she felt otherwise.

"Goot," Jakob exclaimed. "But the treat will be mine. Nothing I like better than to share a meal with friends." He smiled at Ellie. "Especially such pretty friends."

Chapter Ten

"Hey, Leah!" Thomas waved from his perch on one of the rafters of Charley's partially constructed house. "Up here!" Leah and several of her sisters were walking across the yard below. "Leah!"

She looked up, saw him and waved back. Her sisters laughed and waved, as well. "Hold on!" Leah shouted back. "We don't want to have to rush you to the emergency room with a broken leg!"

"I'll try to remember that!" Chuckling, Thomas returned to his task of hammering in a wooden peg, securing one rafter securely to the ridgepole of the house. Heights had never frightened him and he was having the time of his life. From here, it seemed he could see half of Seven Poplars: the chair shop on the other side of the road, Samuel Mast's barn and the brick chimneys of his house, Hannah's house and barns, even Johanna and Roland's farmstead. Working on either side of him were Leah's brothers-in-law Charley and Eli, and two stories below, directing the project, was James Hostetler, a local contractor and carpenter with a lifetime of experience in building houses.

Charley couldn't have picked a better day for the house raising if he'd tried. June was a busy month for farmers, and most of the men who worked in trades outside of Seven Poplars still had work to do on their own farms and homes on weekends. But the entire community and many from other church districts in the county had come to lend a hand on the house. The weather was perfect, temperature in the seventies with clear blue skies. Thomas counted more than twenty men directly involved in the construction, while more carried lumber, sawed wood and assisted the women in setting up the long tables for the midday meal under the trees. He wouldn't even attempt to count the children. The smaller ones were running back and forth and playing, while the older kids were either helping with the coming picnic dinner or running errands for the workmen.

Until now, Charley and his wife had shared a house with one of her sisters, but rumors were that after a long wait, the couple was expecting a second child. Charley's horse breeding and training was a successful sideline to his farming skills, and it was time that his family had room to grow. And, according to tradition, the Amish community and some of the local Englishers had turned out en masse to help. Helping one another was expected. Charley and his wife had done their best to support and aid fellow church members, and now their hard work and dedication would be repaid by their neighbors and friends.

Thomas gave the peg a final blow with his hammer and grinned as it drove without splitting to the depth of the predrilled hole. From below, on the first floor, Albert Hartman, the local veterinarian and Hannah's husband, began the first chorus of an old hymn, and all over the house and yard, men joined in, blending their voices together amid the rhythms and din of hammer and saw. Thomas sang with them, his chest swelling with the warm feelings of unity and faith that united him to these people.

On the far side of the roof, at the top of a ladder, clung Jakob, a huge leather work belt slung over one shoulder and a hammer in his hand. Thomas would have expected Jakob to choose tasks that kept him closer to the ground due to his size, but the little man could climb better than Thomas could.

His strong arms and powerful shoulders made up for his lack of size. Jakob's addition to the family blacksmith shop had, so far, been a resounding success. Thomas knew that his grandfather was pleased with Jakob's work, and the customers all seemed to like him, as well. Jakob started work before breakfast and would continue at the forge until long past the ringing of the supper bell if someone didn't urge him to bank the fire and come to the table.

Thomas moved to another rafter. He glanced up at the sun. Nearly noon. His belly had been grumbling for an hour. House building was hard work. He liked hard work, but he'd been thinking about the feast the women were preparing. He could smell fried chicken, roast beef, *schnitz und knepp,* and baking bread. A pit and turnspit had been prepared and teenage boys had meticulously turned a whole pig for twelve hours over a bed of coals. Thomas could almost taste the juicy slices of pork with its crisp skin and delicious interior. There would be salads, green beans, scalloped potatoes, *kartoffle bolla,* mashed potatoes, buttered beets, stewed tomatoes, English peas with dumplings, cakes, pies and enough gravy to swim in. Every woman would have brought her finest dish, not out of pride but wanting to share her best with her neighbors and family.

"Running short of nails yet?" Jakob called.

Thomas shook his head. "I've got plenty."

"I'm out." Jakob motioned to the area where he was working. "You want to give me a hand with this?"

"No problem." Thomas moved cautiously along the rafter and then walked toward his new friend. "Going good. We should be laying —" His foot slipped and he lost his balance and fell but caught himself with his arms. His heart pounded as he sucked in lungfuls of air, his feet dangling.

"Hang on!" James shouted from below. "Someone will —"

"Got him!" Jakob yelled. He grabbed Thomas by the shirt collar, then the arm, and helped him scramble back up to sit on the narrow beam. "Take your time," Jakob said to Thomas.

"I'm all right." Thomas's heartbeat slowed to somewhere near normal as he glanced down at the distance between where he had just hung and the solid ground far below. He quickly looked back at Jakob. "Whew," he said.

"God is with you," Jakob said. He offered a broad hand, and Thomas took it and slowly rose to his feet. Jakob grinned.

"What's important is that you caught yourself. Back home, I saw a man fall off the roof of a barn and break his back. He lived, but he never walked again, and he had a wife and five children to care for."

"*Ya,* I guess I got a little overconfident." Thomas returned the smile. He couldn't help scanning the dinner area to see if Leah had witnessed his near miss, but she'd been wearing a green dress and he didn't see any. All the women seemed to be clad in various shades of blue, brown and lavender. Several had their heads together and were pointing at the roof, but none of them were his Leah. *Just as well,* he thought.

"Slow and steady works best when you're up this high," Jakob said. "But anybody can slip. Shake it off."

Thomas removed his hat and wiped the sweat off his forehead. His shoulder ached from swinging the hammer, but it was a satisfying twinge. The beam felt solid beneath his feet and he released his death grip on the nearest post and stopped breathing in quick, hard gasps. *God is good,* he thought. And merciful. He swallowed, and attempted to ease his dry throat. "That was a little too close," he said to Jakob.

"But you survived it, and all the girls will be finding an excuse to talk to you during dinner." Jakob grinned again, his high forehead wrinkling with good humor. "And they will be telling you how brave you are. It's almost worth it."

Thomas chuckled. "Only one girl I care to impress. And I don't think she saw me doing my trick."

"A pity," Jakob offered, and they both laughed. And then Jakob said, "How are the baptism classes going?"

"Good. I think." Thomas replaced his hat, tugging it firmly into place. "You already baptized?"

"When I turned eighteen. Back home in Indiana. It was either accept the life or leave home without a penny in my pocket. My father was pretty firm on the subject. But it didn't take much persuasion. I would have come to it in a year or two anyway, once I'd had my fun. This is my faith, and I wouldn't know any other way to live."

"Still, it's a serious decision," Thomas admitted. "Not as easy as I always thought it would be."

Jakob threw him a sympathetic look. "Probably easier when you're younger. You don't consider the magnitude of the decision." He waited and then went on. "But if you have questions or doubts, you don't have to wrestle with them alone. I'd be happy to talk with you, and so would any of the others." He indicated the men working below them.

Thomas nodded. "I appreciate that."

A dinner bell rang loud and clear.

"Guess that's the signal we were waiting for." Jakob started down the ladder. "I don't know about you, but I'm starving."

"I'm not sure I could eat a horse and plow," Thomas replied, following him, "but I could give it a good try." When he reached the bottom floor, Jakob was standing there waiting for him. Other men were descending the ladders, taking off their tool belts, laying down tools, but none were close enough to hear.

"What you said before," Jakob said quietly. "About your concerns. You know we have more than one leader. Preacher Caleb seems sensible. And he's a lot closer to our age than the bishop. You might want to talk to him if you're having any reservations. Now's the time to do it, not after you've joined the church. That's where some make a big mistake."

"It's the practical side that keeps nagging at me," Thomas said as he hung his own tool belt over a nail. "Leah having access to that car, being able to deliver my crop directly to the good markets, that means a lot."

"She's Mennonite, isn't she?"

"Was. Raised Amish but joined the Mennonites when she married. Now she's planning on returning to the faith. She's taking classes, too, the young women's class, of course."

"Are you thinking about becoming Mennonite, instead? Then the two of you could keep the car." Jakob shrugged. "It might be the answer to your dilemma."

"I don't know. That would be a bigger step than going through with the baptism."

Jakob nodded. "*Ya,* but not wrong if your heart leads you in that direction. We choose to live apart from the world, but it's not for everyone. How does Leah feel about it?"

Thomas shrugged. "I don't know. We haven't talked about it."

Jakob paused in the doorway and glanced back at him. "Then you shouldn't be talking to me — you should be discussing it with the woman you intend to marry. It's a decision that you and Leah need to make together."

"You're probably right, but I haven't gotten it straight in my own head. I'm not sure how I feel or what I want. I wasn't sure I should trouble her with the idea until I knew what I wanted." He took off his straw hat again, rolled the brim and slicked back his forelock before replacing the hat.

"There's something in what you're saying," Jakob agreed, "about thinking this through before approaching Leah with it, but —" He broke off and motioned toward the windmill in the yard. "There's your girl, now."

Thomas looked up. It was Leah in her green dress and dainty white lace *kapp*. She was carrying a tray piled high with biscuits, and walking beside her was Ellie, her hands balancing a four-layer chocolate cake.

"A pretty sight," Jakob observed, "those two."

"Leah's taken," Thomas teased. "But Ellie's single and she's not interested in anybody special, not since we broke up."

"That's right. She broke up with you, didn't she?" Jakob asked.

"Turned me down flat when I asked her to marry me."

Jakob laughed. "Shows what good sense she has. I have a feeling she was waiting for me to show up in town."

Leah saw them approaching and smiled. Ellie frowned, turned on her heels and marched back in the direction from which she had come.

"I don't know about that. She doesn't seem all that infatuated with you," Thomas teased.

"Don't believe it. She adores me. Who wouldn't?" Jakob threw out his arms in a dramatic gesture. "I'm handsome. Hardworking. And very modest."

Thomas chuckled at his antics. "Ellie can be tough, but she's going to make someone a fine wife. Don't give up on her if you're interested."

"I'm not giving up on the pretty little schoolteacher," Jakob replied, still watching Ellie retreat. "She had me from the first time I laid eyes on her. She's going to be my wife. She just doesn't know it yet."

"Ellie? Where are you going?" Leah called.

Rebecca came up behind Leah. "Let me take those biscuits. *Mam* wants you to fill the water glasses. There's a pitcher on the side table over there."

"Like old times, isn't it?" Leah smiled at her sister as she handed her the tray. "When we were all living at home. *Mam* always took charge, even when it wasn't her dinner."

Rebecca laughed. "*Mam* hasn't changed, Leah, and neither have you. The trouble is, the two of you are too much alike. I think you both like to give orders." Her dimples flashed as she smiled. "It's so good to have you back with us again."

"Good to be back." Leah brushed her sister's cheek with a kiss. "I have to admit, I did miss your pointing out my failings."

"See?" Rebecca laughed again. "I am good for something."

When they were small, they'd always joined together as a team making a united front against Miriam, Johanna, Anna and Ruth, who'd seemed so grown-up and in charge. Leah had never doubted that all of her sisters loved her and would come to her aid if she needed them, but she had to admit, for all her ideas, Rebecca was her favorite. "You really think I'm like our mother?"

"Absolutely," Rebecca pronounced. "*Mam* even says so herself. And you know she's rarely wrong."

"We need biscuits at this end of table!" their sister Ruth called.

Rebecca rolled her eyes. "A woman's work is never done."

"It's hardly work, though," Leah answered. "More of a holiday with everyone here."

Rebecca nudged her with an elbow. "There's your Thomas over there with the new blacksmith. They're watching you, or at least Thomas is."

"*Ne,* he's not," Leah replied, although she knew he was. "He's just hungry for his dinner. Thomas is always ready to eat." Just saying his name made her want to laugh. She saw him almost every day, but still, seeing him here today was exciting. It made her feel like a giddy teenager again.

"You're blushing," Rebecca teased.

"*Ne,* I'm not."

"There's nothing to be ashamed of. Thomas and you will make a wonderful couple, and you'll be a beautiful bride. Don't you remember how it was when you met Daniel? You were so happy. I'm glad to see you happy again."

Leah pressed her lips together, suddenly feeling a twinge of guilt. It wasn't the same as Daniel. It couldn't be. No one could take Daniel's place in her heart. It wasn't possible. "It's not like that with me and Thomas," she protested. "Not the same at all. I told you this weeks ago. Thomas and I are marrying because it makes sense. He needs a wife. I need a husband and this is the solution."

Rebecca set the tray of biscuits on the long table, grabbed Leah's arm and tugged her aside. "Come with me," she said, walking away from the bustling women and children.

"Did I hear you say what I thought I did?" She didn't stop until they were partially hidden by a large lilac bush. "Are you telling me you don't love Thomas?"

Leah shook off her sister's hand on her arm. "Sara arranged this match. It's not . . . It was never supposed to be romantic. I told you that."

"I know what you told me when you started seeing each other, but I assumed things had changed between you and Thomas." Rebecca held Leah's gaze. "You've certainly been acting like things have changed." She lowered her voice. "I thought you were in love with him."

Leah squared her shoulders. "I like Thomas. I respect him. But our relationship is about companionship . . . friendship. Not everyone who marries is madly, romantically in love with each other."

Rebecca frowned, crossing her arms over her chest. "Maybe it's too soon for you to be thinking of marriage. Maybe you need longer to mourn what you've lost. Give yourself more time. You loved Daniel so much. I wouldn't rush into marriage again if you're not ready, because that would be a mistake. And unfair to Thomas."

"I'm not making a mistake. Thomas understands. I told him from the first my reasons for wanting to marry again."

"All right, if you're sure." Rebecca sighed, looking unconvinced. "You know I just want what's best for you. Remember what happened with Johanna. She thought she was in love with Wilmer and look how that turned out."

Leah sighed and stared at her bare feet. "Thomas is not Wilmer. They are nothing alike, and I'm not Johanna. I know what I'm doing. Don't worry about me."

"It's just that I care about you, and I want you to be happy."

"I am happy," Leah insisted.

Rebecca looked at her.

"I *am,*" Leah repeated, opening her arms wide.

Seeming to sense she'd pushed hard enough, Rebecca changed the subject. "How are the baptismal classes going?"

"Good."

"And Thomas's?" Rebecca asked.

"Okay, I suppose." She grimaced, knowing that she could never deceive Rebecca. "The truth is, I think he's struggling a little."

"Second thoughts?"

"Nothing like that. I think it's just that he's been a bachelor for so long, having fun, avoiding responsibility, that taking classes with the bishop means that this is for real."

"It's not cold feet? Because I'd hate for you to be the one dumped after everyone has planted fields of celery for your wedding."

Leah rolled her eyes. "Thomas is not dumping me." She shook her head. "It's not about me. I think he's just a little nervous, is all. About the responsibilities of a man in our community."

"And you've talked about it?"

"We talk all the time," Leah assured her.

"Leah! Rebecca!" Miriam appeared around the corner of the house. "What are the two of you doing over here? *Mam*'s been looking for you. The food is ready for the first sitting. And Thomas is looking for you, too, Leah." She glanced over her shoulder. "Over here, Thomas." Miriam looked back at Leah. "Did you see him almost take that dive off the roof?"

"What?" Leah asked.

"Scared me half to death." She brought her hand to her heart. "He fell off one of the roof rafters."

"Nothing for you to get upset about," Thomas assured her as he joined them. "It was a stupid mistake on my part. I caught myself." He waved one hand. "No harm done."

Stunned, Leah stared at him. He'd almost

fallen off the roof? She struggled to draw a breath. "But . . . but you're all right?" she asked, feeling a little light-headed. "You caught yourself? You didn't fall?"

He grinned boyishly. "*Ne.* I didn't fall far. Didn't even get a scratch."

She had an impulse to run to him and hug him, but she couldn't. Not with her sisters both standing there.

But she wanted to hug him. She wanted to hold him tight. Which she found a bit bewildering. She'd just told her sister she didn't have romantic feelings for Thomas, and here she was, wanting to throw herself into his arms. Everything she had said to Rebecca made perfect sense. It was this feeling in her stomach, in her heart, that was confusing.

Leah forced a smile. "You must be hungry," she said to Thomas. "For . . . dinner. Dinner's ready."

The last bell for the first seating rang.

"You'd best get to the table," she said hastily. "Before grace." She looked at her sisters. "And we . . . we need to get back to work." Without waiting for Thomas to respond, she rushed off toward the kitchen. She needed to think this out, and she couldn't think when Thomas was around.

Later, she promised herself. Later, she'd figure all this out.

CHAPTER ELEVEN

By nine thirty Saturday morning the pancake breakfast at the Mennonite church was in full swing. Leah stood at the six-burner stove in the big kitchen flipping pancakes, while Daniel's aunt Joyce stirred up another batch of batter. The cheerful room, with its large windows overlooking picnic tables and a children's playground, was buzzing with activity. Caroline, Aunt Joyce's daughter, was loading the commercial dishwasher while her sister Leslie poured orange juice and another woman, Gwen, wiped down the counters. Eight-year-old Yasmin, another of Daniel's cousins, darted in and out of the kitchen carrying napkins and fresh jugs of maple syrup.

Daniel and his aunt had been close, and Joyce had always been kind and welcoming to Leah. So when Aunt Joyce asked her to help with the fundraiser for the Mennonite school, Leah was only too happy to pitch in. When Thomas heard she was going, he offered to go, too, saying he liked the idea of seeing what her life had been like as a Mennonite woman. Everyone at the church had been pleased to have an extra set of hands and Thomas had immediately been put to work serving the breakfasts with the other men. Always the good sport, he hadn't even complained when Aunt Joyce had tied an oversize white apron around him.

"We're just waiting for the final approval from the court," Aunt Joyce said, continuing with her update on the impending adoption of her foster child, Yasmin. "We applied over a year ago, after she came to live with us, but there's a great-grandmother objecting to the placement. Yasmin lived with her when she was an infant, but the grandmother is elderly and in poor health. Social Services thinks our adoption application will still be approved, but the process is slow."

"The entire church is praying for your family," Gwen said as she sprayed the counter with cleaner. "You can see how happy the child is. When she first came she was so shy and withdrawn she hardly said a word to anyone. Look at her now."

"I'll keep you in my prayers," Leah assured Joyce.

"As you remain in ours." Joyce turned on

the mixer. When the contents of the bowl were sufficiently blended, she carried the pancake batter to the stove. "We expect another run soon," she said. "The Janzen family hasn't arrived yet, and they said they were bringing their neighbors."

Leah nodded. "I'll get started on another batch, but we can pop them in the warm oven when they're done. We don't want to serve anyone a cold breakfast." She smiled. "And who knows, the Janzens all might want bacon and eggs instead of pancakes." She used a spatula to remove the pancakes that were done and slid them onto serving-sized plates as Thomas came in through the swinging doors, carrying an empty tray.

"Three more for pancakes," he said.

Leah turned to look at him. His straw hat was pushed up on his forehead, and his name tag hung precariously from one strap of the apron. "Were any of the guests surprised to find their waiter was Amish?" she teased as she dried her hands on her apron and approached him to straighten his name tag.

Thomas shrugged. "If they were, they had the good manners to not say so. Except for one little boy, who asked me if my mama hadn't taught me to take my hat off in the house."

She adjusted his name tag, smiling up at him. "What did you say?"

"What could I say?" Thomas grinned. "I told him that I was carrying food and had to keep my hat on or wear a hairnet."

"Good answer. You can take those." She stepped back, indicating the pancakes she'd just taken off the griddle.

Thomas scooped up the big oval plate that had both blueberry and plain pancakes on it and deposited it on the tray, then reached for a serving plate of bacon. He grinned and winked at her as he hurried back out of the kitchen with the tray. Leah couldn't help chuckling. Some Amish men were uncomfortable with women's work, but not Thomas. She liked that about him; he reminded her of her father, who had not been above grabbing a dishcloth and helping wash dishes after supper.

Leah walked back to the stove and used a ladle to pour more batter onto the hot griddle. As she replaced the bowl on the counter she made eye contact with Aunt Joyce. To her puzzlement, her usually good-natured aunt was frowning. "What's wrong?" Leah asked.

Aunt Joyce shook her head. "Later."

Leah glanced around the kitchen. Everyone was still working steadily. Had she missed something? "Aunt Joyce —"

"Later, dear," Aunt Joyce repeated, and turned her attention to putting away a stack of clean dishes.

The older woman's odd behavior nagged at Leah, though, and when Joyce headed outside to carry scraps of food to the compost bin, Leah followed her. "Aunt Joyce," she said, quickening her step to keep up with the older woman. "Have I said something to upset you?"

Joyce stopped, considered Leah and took a deep breath. "It's simply that . . . I have to tell you that it pains me to see your behavior with that young man. It's . . . not appropriate, Leah."

"What behavior's not 'appropriate'?" she asked, trying not to get her feathers ruffled. "What did I do?"

"Making eyes at him, of course. And . . . touching him. All the flirting. I'm not a prude, Leah. I was young once. But you aren't a girl. You're a widow. In my mind, you shouldn't be putting your hands on a man not your husband. It's not a good example for the younger ones in our congregation. Or in our family. It's clear to me that you're besotted with the boy. The two of you are as giggly with each other as a pair of teenagers."

"I'm sorry," Leah said, crushed at the criticism. "I didn't even realize I'd —" Then she remembered she *had* adjusted Thomas's name tag a few minutes earlier in the kitchen. And when he'd untied her apron strings in fun, their fingers might have caught for just a moment. But nothing had been *inappropriate*. And she'd certainly not been *making eyes* at him. "Aunt Joyce, I'm sorry. I thought you knew that Thomas and I are courting." Courting couples were generally given more leeway in their behavior because a couple who announces a courtship is announcing their intentions to marry if all goes well.

"Courting, are you?" Joyce sniffed.

Leah softened her tone, wondering if she hadn't been as considerate of Aunt Joyce's feelings as she should have. Maybe it had been a mistake to bring Thomas. "It's been over a year since Daniel died. My family and I agree it's time I marry again. It's what Daniel wanted." She hesitated. "Do you think it's too soon?"

Joyce's brow wrinkled. "Of course not," she answered tersely. "No one expects a widow of your age to remain alone. It wouldn't be natural. But . . ." She stiffened and walked on purposefully. The church was deeply concerned with earth-friendly practices and had installed a series of covered bins along the wall of a storage shed. Food scraps went into a compost bin that was turned regularly to produce clean garden soil. Joyce lifted the lid and deposited the contents of her bucket. "I'm just going to come out and say this, dear. It's fine that you remarry. It's your duty. But it isn't . . . it just isn't respectful to Daniel to take up with someone like Thomas."

" 'Someone like Thomas'?" Leah repeated, having no idea what she meant.

"I have nothing against Thomas," Joyce said with a sharp nod of her chin. "He's quite likable, in fact. Witty. A handsome face. So full of life." She leaned closer. "Which makes him totally unsuitable," she said, lowering her voice, "for a second marriage."

"What do you mean?"

"I mean there's nothing wrong with following one's heart's desires, a *body's inclinations,* the first time around. But out of respect for your deceased husband and for his family," she said pointedly, "you need someone more appropriate. A woman in your position doesn't marry for love."

"I'm not in love with Thomas," Leah argued. "This is an arrangement made by a matchmaker."

"You should come to supper tomorrow night," Joyce went on, not seeming to have heard her. "There's someone I want you to meet, a member of our church. Eldon Goosen. He's older, a widower with children who need a mother, and he's asked about you. He thinks you seem like a good worker. Eldon's going to Poland to take up a mission in July or August. Plenty of time for the two of you to become acquainted. And an excellent second marriage for both of you."

Leah took a step back, feeling a little numb. What would make Aunt Joyce think she was in love with Thomas? "A Mennonite man won't do. I've decided to become Amish again. It's important to my family and to me. I've already started my classes. I'll be baptized in late summer."

Aunt Joyce frowned. "Fine. Then surely there's an appropriate Amish widower looking for someone to cook and clean for him. Someone with a readymade family. It's best you leave young men like Thomas to women who've not yet had a husband."

Leah glanced down at the grass, not sure how to respond to that. "I . . . I'd better get back to making pancakes." She turned away. "We wouldn't want anyone waiting too long."

"Just think on what I've said, Leah," Joyce called after her.

All Leah could do was nod and hurry away.

A few nights later, Thomas stopped by Sara's after dinner. Leah and Sara were sitting on the porch with Hiram, Sara's hired man, Ellie and Florence, a young woman from New York State who'd come to Delaware to be married.

Leah got to her feet as Thomas came up the steps. Ever since her conversation with Daniel's aunt, she'd been feeling out of sorts. Not with Thomas, but with herself, though why, she wasn't quite sure. "Ellie just made lemonade," she said. "Would you like some? Or a slice of chocolate pie?"

"The pie sounds good." Thomas nodded a greeting to Sara and the others. "But it's such a nice evening. I was hoping you might like to take a walk with me." He glanced at Sara. "Maybe I could have that slice of pie when we get back."

"If Hiram doesn't get to it first." Sara stroked the gray cat curled in her lap.

Hiram's face reddened and he ducked his head. "A man can't help it if you make a good pie. A man can't help it if he likes good pie."

212

"Would you listen to that?" Sara teased. "Hiram just said more than ten words in one stretch. Better keep an eye on the weather, Thomas. It might just snow."

"Needn't take on so," Hiram muttered. "I'm a man of few words, unlike some around here." He threw a look Thomas's way.

Thomas chuckled. "True enough, Hiram." He glanced at Leah. "What do you say? Do you feel like a walk?"

"Sure," Leah agreed.

Thomas looked back at Sara. "You're welcome to come along," he offered. "If you'd like to chaperone."

Sara shook her head. "I've been on these feet too long today." She wiggled her bare toes. "I'm content to sit right here, enjoy this lemonade and tease Hiram. You two go on and enjoy yourselves. But behave. I've got my eye on you, Thomas. You know I do."

Leah followed Thomas off the porch and into the yard. "Where did you want to walk?"

What Daniel's aunt had said at the pancake breakfast had troubled her, but she hadn't mentioned the conversation to Thomas. It seemed disloyal to tell him that Joyce was trying to match her with a Mennonite widower. She wouldn't want Thomas

213

to think that she'd consider it. But Joyce's words lingered in the back of her mind and nagged at her until seeds of doubt sprouted. Joyce's suggestion that Leah was marrying Thomas because she had fallen in love with him was ridiculous. As ridiculous as her insinuation that Leah was stealing a young, good-looking man from younger girls better deserving.

Leah matched her pace with Thomas's and they walked without speaking through the late shadows of the day out of the farmyard and down the back lane. The weather was perfect with just a slight breeze that kept the mosquitoes away. They passed through a gate and strolled across the back pasture where the mules grazed in the light of the setting sun, and on to the edge of the wood line, where Thomas stopped her with a quick gesture. Leah stood absolutely still and watched in delight as a wild turkey hen strolled out of the trees, followed by a line of babies. The turkey poults were about the size of doves, miniatures of their mother and so cute. They trailed the mother in perfect formation, one after another, staring around with bright eyes and imitating her as she pecked at the ground.

After a few minutes of watching the birds, Thomas abruptly clapped his hands together. At the sound, the turkeys flew up, exploding up in a flurry of feathers and long necks, and then flapped and darted into the woods.

"*Ach!* Why did you frighten them away?" Leah asked.

"I didn't want the little ones to become too accustomed to us. If they're not afraid of people, they'll end up on someone's table." He shrugged. "I warn you, I'm not much of a hunter."

She smiled at him. "I'm glad. I always felt sorry for the animals that the St. Joes hunted in the jungle. Monkeys, sloths, turtles. I didn't blame them because I knew they needed meat to feed their families, but it made me sad to see them come home with dead creatures hanging from poles."

"You have a gentle heart, Leah."

"Or a foolish one. I grew up on a farm. I know where hamburger and fried chicken comes from. But I still hate to see wild things killed." She peered into the woods, half-expecting to see the bright flash of parrot feathers or hear the haunting cry of a jaguar. But the jungle was faraway. And so were the graves she'd left there. She turned back into the light. "I'm glad we saw the turkeys," she said. "I think they're beautiful."

"*Ya,* I think so, too." He smiled, turning to face her. "You don't see them often." He gazed into her eyes. "But that's not all that's pretty out here."

She looked away, her cheeks warm, but she didn't protest when Thomas took her hand and kissed the back of it. "I'll take care of you, you know," he said quietly. He raised her hand to his face and pressed it against his chin.

Leah shivered as she felt the prickle of a new growth of beard. Thomas had shaved that morning. She knew because he shaved every morning, but his dark hair and beard grew quickly. Once they were married, it would be easy for him to grow a full beard. She thought it would make him even more handsome.

"I want you to know that," he continued. "You'll never go hungry or lack a roof over your head. I'll work hard, you can count on it." He unfolded her hand and ran fingertips over her palm. "I love your hands," he confided. "Such small hands, but so strong and graceful."

Leah felt herself blush. She pulled her hand free, conscious of the nails broken by gardening and the one thumbnail she'd bitten to the quick. "You're sweet to say so," she managed, "but my hands are a mess."

English girls, she knew, often had their nails polished, but she was content when hers were clean and sensibly shaped. She rubbed lotion into her hands every night after her bath, but canning, housework and outside chores often left them callused and reddened.

"I think your hands are beautiful," Thomas insisted. "And not just your hands. All of you. I always thought you were the prettiest girl I'd ever known."

"Stop." She looked at the grass at their feet. "You're embarrassing me. You shouldn't say such things. You'll make me vain."

"*Ne,* Leah. Not you. I wanted you to know . . . that I think so. That you're beautiful. And good. And I want you to know how much I care for you, because . . ." He lowered his gaze. "Because we haven't talked about our feelings . . . for each other."

She didn't know what to say. She didn't want to talk about her feelings for Thomas because she was so confused. Her plan had been a good one: a matchmaker, a marriage of convenience. What she hadn't planned on was this man she'd known her whole life who'd brought laughter into her heart again.

He leaned down and picked a tiny bouquet of wild violets from the moss at the edge of the trees and pressed it into her hand. "I'll plant flowers in my garden just for you. Would you like that?"

"I would," she admitted. "I love flowers." She raised the violets to her nose and sniffed the sweetness, thinking they should start back.

"You know," Thomas ventured, looking down at her. "I almost think I should do what Sara told me not to."

"What's that?" She looked up at him and, before she realized what he was about to do, before she could react, he leaned close.

His lips brushed hers, resting there for just a few seconds, caressing and tender. For an instant, it felt strange. No man had ever kissed her before, except for Daniel. She wanted to pull away, to tell him no, but the warmth and the sweet touch of his mouth was more than she could resist.

It was Thomas who released her and stepped back. Which was a good thing because she didn't know if she'd have had the strength to do it. She felt breathless, and her knees were unsteady.

"That was nice."

She touched her lips with a fingertip and smiled at him. "Too nice," she murmured, taking a step back and then another. She had known the kissing would come. Certainly in their marriage bed, but it hadn't occurred to her that she would like it so much. Suddenly the world felt off-kilter and she could barely find her voice. "I think we better go back."

Thomas chuckled. "*Ya,* we better." He took her hand and she let him, and they started back the way they'd come. "But I've been wanting to talk to you about something."

"Okay," Leah heard herself say.

"It's about my baptism classes. My joining the church."

She looked up at him, trying to move past the kiss. Talking was better. "You said they were going well."

"They are. I just . . . I've been wondering about something, Leah."

She stopped to give him her full attention. "What's that?"

"Well, I wondered if maybe we're going about this all wrong. Maybe this isn't what we were meant to do."

"I don't understand."

"I'm talking about both of us being baptized in the Amish church. Maybe . . ." He seemed to be struggling to find the right words. "Leah, do you think you should consider staying Mennonite and I should join the Mennonite church?"

She stared at him, thinking she must have misheard. "You want to become Mennonite?"

"I don't know. That's what I'm saying. Do we need to rethink this? If I became Mennonite, we could keep the car or even buy a truck for the deliveries. I assumed you would become Amish to marry me, but what's to say I shouldn't join your faith instead of you having to change yours for me?" He gazed earnestly into her eyes. "What do you think, Leah?"

CHAPTER TWELVE

Leah stepped back and stared at him with a horrified expression. "You want to abandon your faith?"

"I didn't say that," Thomas protested. "I've just been thinking and I wondered if it was fair to you to —"

"You *knew* that I wanted to become Amish again," Leah interrupted, the anger in her tone startling him. "It's why I came to Sara for a husband." She threw up her arms. "I don't believe this. Why do you think I'm going to baptismal classes?"

Thomas stood there for a moment, stunned. Had he known she was going to react this strongly, he'd have never brought it up. It was just that everyone was encouraging him to talk with Leah about things. "I'm not saying it's what we *have* to do," he defended. "I just . . . I thought we should talk about it. Sara said it's important for couples to — it was just something I thought about and wanted to —" And again, before he could finish what he was trying to say, she lashed back at him.

"*Ne*. I don't want to hear any more." She held up her hand. "It's not what I want. It's not what I agreed to. I won't agree to it. I won't marry you." She folded her arms and stared at him with brimming eyes.

Remorse swept over him, making his gut clench. "Don't say that, Leah. I love you. I want you to be my wife. I'll do whatever you —"

"*Ne*. No more." She whirled around and walked away from him, then stopped and glanced back. "You would give up our whole way of life for the sake of a car?" Her lips puckered as if she'd tasted something bitter. "Being able to drive means more to you than sitting in worship with our families? Than raising children in our fathers' faith?"

He could feel his own temper rising. She was being unfair. That wasn't what he'd said. It certainly wasn't what he'd meant. He was thinking of her more than anything. And he hadn't said he wanted to become Mennonite — he'd only said the idea had crossed his mind. Why was she acting like this? He had just wanted to talk this thing out with her. "There's no need to overreact. I was just asking."

"Don't tell me how I should feel, Thomas!" She shook her head adamantly.

"I think we both need to cool down and discuss this calmly," he said, walking toward her.

"What is there to talk about? I know what I want. And clearly, you don't. So this is not going to work. I won't marry you, Thomas. I thought we . . ." She shook her head again. "It doesn't matter. We obviously don't want the same things in life."

"You're behaving irrationally, Leah. You don't walk away from what we've found together because we've had a disagreement." He gestured with one hand. "This isn't even a disagreement. I just wanted to talk it over with you."

She continued to shake her head. "I'm sorry, but it's over between us. Find someone else, a girl who wants motor cars and electricity. I'm not that woman."

Leah raised her foot from the pedal of her mother's old Singer sewing machine and glanced up from the seam she was finishing. "This is good material," she said to her mother. "It's been so long since I've worked with anything this nice. At the mission, I had to put in a request for cloth and hope that I got something close to what I needed." She'd left her own sewing machine behind when she'd returned to the United States. The family that replaced her would have a greater need than she would.

"I'm glad you like the ticking," her mother said. "It's so nice to have all of you girls here and working together on the pillows. Just like old times."

"It is, isn't it?" Leah agreed. When Rebecca had stopped by Sara's that morning to ask her to come, Leah had been thankful for the invitation. She'd always liked making pillows. Hannah was one of the few women who still made them the old-fashioned way. All year, she and Johanna saved down from their geese for stuffing. It took a lot of work, but the resulting pillows would last for years. Best of all, it was a great excuse to get together with her sisters and mother, to laugh and share the latest family news.

It was just what she needed after the awful breakup with Thomas earlier in the week . . . the breakup she still hadn't told anyone about.

She just hadn't been ready to answer the questions she would be asked. She had no right to repeat Thomas's doubts about remaining in the faith. That was private and personal, not something to be discussed by the community until he made a final decision. But she was glad he'd come to her when he did because there was no need to drag out their courtship if it wasn't going anywhere.

Maybe her dreams of remarrying were just that. Dreams. Maybe she wasn't meant to find happiness in another marriage, or to be a mother again. She had other options. She knew that she could find a home with *Mam* or any of her sisters. Someone would have to care for Susanna and David when her mother and Albert grew older. Could it be that God meant for her to spend her life caring for her little sister and helping her family? She could still return to the church, still be with those she loved.

She sighed and returned to the seam she'd been reinforcing on the pillow casing. The dull ache that had haunted her since her confrontation with Thomas threatened to ruin the day. Just as it had ruined the previous day.

And the one before.

She steeled herself to not allow her regrets to drag her down. She could withstand this disappointment. Prayer and faith would carry her until the pain of losing Thomas faded.

A flash of blue and flying pigtails caught

her attention, yanking her from her thoughts. Anna's small daughter Rose darted across the sewing room and thrust chubby hands into the basket containing the goose down.

Giggling, she seized handfuls of down feathers and tossed them into the air. "Snow!" she shrieked in *Deitsch*. "Snow!"

"*Leibchen,* how did you get in here?" Anna laughed as she laid down the embroidered pillowcase she was hemming and scooped up her little daughter. "Ruth, can you come get this escapee?"

Leah's throat constricted at the sight of her sister and child. So beautiful, she thought. Did Anna have any notion of how fortunate she was? Goose down settled on the child's butter-yellow hair and clung to her blue dress, a perfect copy of the one Anna wore, complete with white apron. Anna had braided Rose's hair into two tiny plaits secured by ties of white ribbon, plaits that stuck out on either side of her perfectly shaped head.

Hannah laughed. "She loves to be in the center of the action, don't you, pumpkin? Give her to me, Anna. *Grossmama* will tend to her."

Anna passed her daughter over and Hannah took a clump of down out of the child's hair and tickled her nose with it. Rose giggled and patted Hannah's cheeks.

"Thirsty," Rose said. "Want milk."

"Do you?" Hannah asked. "How about if you come down to the kitchen with me and we'll fix a snack for you and your cousins?"

Rose's head bobbed in agreement. *"Ya."*

"Goot," Anna said. "You go and help *Grossmama*. And stay downstairs. I don't know how you got away from your aunt Ruth."

Susanna and Ruth had taken the children into the front room, where they were playing with an assortment of wooden blocks and farm animals that Albert had carved for them. Usually Rose was quite happy bossing Ruth's twin boys around and feeding cookies to Miriam's little son or rocking one of the babies, but she had an independent streak and was as mischievous as Rebecca had been as a child. No stranger, looking at those innocent blue eyes, red cheeks and sweet lips, would suspect Rose of being the ringleader of her nephews' troublemaking.

"You think I'm joking," Anna said to Leah when their mother had led Rose out of the sewing room. "She's a handful. Mashed potatoes in her father's work boots, kittens in the bread box and coloring all over her father's latest copy of *The Budget.* And that's just since the Sabbath."

"But she has a good heart," Rebecca defended. "No one could be more gentle with the babies. And she can't stand to see the boys squabbling. She never cries if she falls and skins her knee, but she wept a bucket of tears over one of the chicks that died hatching out of its egg."

"Samuel would spoil her rotten, if I let him. And the older children give in to her. It was one thing when she was a baby," Anna said, taking up her needle again and searching for a spool of thread, "but I'll do her no favors if I let her do as she pleases."

Leah smoothed out the pillow casing and examined the double line of stitching. "I still can't get used to hearing *Mam* refer to herself as *Grossmama.* I keep thinking that she's talking about *Dat*'s mother."

Anna nodded. "I would have liked to bring her with me today. I think she would have enjoyed being with us. But she's failing. The doctor says her heart is weak. She sleeps a lot."

"I'll come to see her tomorrow," Leah promised. She felt guilty. She hadn't spent much time with *Grossmama* since she'd come home. "*Mam* said that she'd gotten very quiet, but I didn't realize that she had serious health problems."

"Other than her wandering mind, you mean?" Rebecca put in. "I don't think she knows who Anna is anymore. She's always calling her Hannah."

Leah grimaced. "Is she cross with you?" she asked Anna. She and their *mam* never got along very well.

Anna shook her head. "*Ne.* I think she lives in her own world most of the time. She likes to sit and rock in that big chair by the window. Sometimes she hums hymns, but mostly she sleeps. I don't think we'll have her with us long."

"She hasn't gone to the Senior Center in months," Rebecca said. "She used to teach other women how to make rugs, but she's not able to do that anymore. She wants her sewing bag beside her chair, but she doesn't open it. It makes me sad. I think I'd rather have her fussing at us."

"The Lord will take her in His own time," Anna said. "Samuel has talked about bringing one of his cousin's daughters here to help me if *Grossmama* can't get to the bathroom on her own. He's so good with her." Anna smiled. "She thinks he is our father, and Samuel doesn't tell her different. He can coax her to eat when none of us can. I was truly blessed to find such a husband."

"*Ya,*" Rebecca agreed. "Samuel is the best of men." She stuffed another handful of down into a bulging pillow casing. "Best of all, he cherishes you, Anna."

Anna's full cheeks flushed a deeper red. "Such things you say."

"It's true, everyone knows it," Rebecca insisted. "And it's no more than you deserve."

Leah took another length of material and began on a new pillowcase. From downstairs came the sounds of children's high-pitched voices and her mother's laughter. She was so glad that she'd come today. Being in her mother's house, in the place where she'd grown up, in the bosom of her family, was just what she needed.

"Can I ask you something?" she said, looking at Anna.

Her older sister smiled. "You know you can ask me anything."

"When you and Samuel married, were you sure he was the one God intended for you?" Leah folded the casing and averted her gaze.

Anna gave a hearty laugh. "Absolutely. I couldn't believe that a man like Samuel would care for me."

"But why not?" Leah asked. True, Anna was a big woman, round and healthy and plain as rye bread. But her heart was the most generous of any of her sisters, and she was as good a cook, mother and homemaker as their mother. "Why wouldn't Samuel love you?"

Anna's cheeks reddened and her round face creased into a bashful grin. "Oh, my little sister, that you should ask. I was a fat girl with a face like a pudding. *Ne,* don't try to argue. No one ever called me pretty, and with good reason. But God was good and he sent me a wonderful husband and children to love. And I know that He will do the same for you. I know that you and Thomas will —"

"I don't want to talk about Thomas," Leah said, looking down.

"But we have to," Rebecca said. "At least we have to talk about your wedding. Have you picked a date?"

Leah shook her head, afraid to look up at her sisters for fear she would start to cry. "I've need to tell you . . . Thomas and I have —"

A giggle came from the doorway. "Leah loves Thomas." Susanna walked into the room with a plate of whoopie pies. "Chocolate." Obviously, Susanna had already tasted the oversize cookies because she had crumbs on the front of her dress and at the corners of her mouth. She giggled again. "Leah and Thomas getting married. Like me and King David."

Leah's throat tightened and her eyes welled with tears. "*Ne.* We're not."

"Not what?" Rebecca asked.

"Not . . . getting . . . married," Leah managed to say between sobs. She jumped up, letting the ticking material fall to the floor unheeded. Clapping her hands over her face, she ran from the room and down the hall to her old bedroom. She dashed inside, slamming the door behind her and threw herself on the double bed. She pulled a pillow over her head to muffle her weeping, but it did no good.

All three of her sisters followed her into the bedroom. Susanna, who could never stand to see anyone cry, began to wail herself. Rebecca tried to comfort Susanna while Anna sat on the bed beside Leah and pulled her into her arms.

"Leah, Leah, what is it?" Anna asked. "What's wrong?"

"Nothing," Leah sobbed.

"Something certainly is wrong," Anna said.

Susanna dissolved into tears again. "Don't . . . don't cry, Leah."

Leah sat up and wiped her eyes. "I'm

sorry." Anna's arms were strong and warm, and she leaned against her sister. "Thomas and . . . I . . . we . . ."

"You argued. It happens." Rebecca sat on the other side of the bed. "What did you quarrel about?"

"It doesn't matter," Leah said. "I can't marry him. We broke up."

"Have you told *Mam*?" Anna asked her. "You have to tell *Mam*."

"*Ne*. I can't." Leah sniffed. "I don't want to."

Rebecca stroked her arm. "All couples have spats," she said. "You can talk it out. In a day or two, this will be behind you."

"It won't," Leah said, fresh tears welling in her eyes. "It's over. I can't explain. But neither can I be his wife. Not now, not ever."

"Whoa, whoa." Thomas took a firm grip on the halter and soothed the nervous bay horse. "Easy, boy. This won't hurt." The gelding rolled his eyes. He laid his ears back and shifted his weight from one leg to another. "Careful," Thomas warned Jakob. "He might kick."

"Not if I can get this leg up, he won't," the little man answered.

Smoke rose from the forge, curling up to lie thick beneath the roof of the smithy. It

233

was raining out and they'd had to bring the horse inside to shoe him. The confines of the building made it all the more important that they keep the animal under control. Had it been up to Thomas, they would have taken him across the yard to the barn and done the work in a stall, but Jakob assured him that they could manage here.

"The horse will be fine," Jakob said. "He just likes to act up a little to show us who's boss. Once we convince him otherwise, he'll calm down."

"I could blindfold him," Thomas offered. It was an old trick of his grandfather's for dealing with skittish animals.

"*Ne,* no need." Jakob stroked the horse's rump and spoke to the animal in a soft, singsong voice. He ran his hands down the gelding's hip and leg, then pressed his weight against the horse as he lifted the back hoof. The horse gave a nervous snort, caught its balance on three legs and stood still. "See, what did I tell you?" Jakob said. He pried away the old shoe and cast it aside. With a curved knife, he trimmed the hoof, traded that tool for a pick and cleaned the hoof.

Thomas scratched under the horse's chin. "Good boy," he repeated. The animal's nostrils flared and he trembled, but he didn't make any attempt to break free.

"I took the wagon down to the chair shop to pick up a chest of drawers for your grandmother," Jakob said. "And who do you suppose was there to use the telephone?"

Thomas sighed. "I can guess."

"That pretty little schoolteacher, that's who." Jakob fitted the new shoe against the hoof. "She pretended not to see me, but I know better. I offered to give her a ride home in the wagon."

"And what did she say to that?"

Jakob laughed. "She likes me. I can tell. But she's a lot like this horse. Trying to bluff me. You were right. She's tough. But she'll come around."

"You think so, do you?" Thomas chuckled.

"Why wouldn't she? Now that you're getting hitched, how many handsome, charming single men are there left in Seven Poplars?"

"Including yourself in that group, are you?"

"Truth's truth, Thomas. I'm a catch, if I do say so myself. I'll make a fine husband. And I've decided that Ellie's the one."

"Not doing too good so far, are you?"

"No need to be negative," Jakob said, driving the first nail into the horse's hoof. "The Lord helps those who help themselves. I've got plans."

"I can't wait to hear them."

"You and Leah are getting married. Between you, you're related to most of the people in the county. It will be a big wedding and you'll need lots of attendants. I'd like to offer my services to be one. Since Leah and Ellie are friends, Leah is bound to ask her. I'll arrange to have us paired off together for the work and later, sitting together at the wedding dinner." Jakob grinned. "Nothing like a wedding to make a young woman inclined to think of love."

"Just one problem with your plan," Thomas said, rubbing the gelding's nose. His voice sounded strange in his own ears. "Leah and I aren't getting married."

"What happened? Don't tell me you're getting cold feet? You can't stay a bachelor forever, you know. Leah's perfect for you."

"*Ne,* apparently not. She was the one who broke it off with me."

Jakob's voice tightened. "You didn't get fresh with her, did you?"

"Of course not," Thomas said. "Who do you think I am?"

"A fool if you don't marry her."

"I'm telling you. She won't have me."

"Why not? What happened?"

Thomas shook his head. "I don't really

know. I . . . I was trying to talk to her about something. You know . . . kind of wanting to think something through out loud and she just . . . she got really angry with me. Flew right off the handle, which isn't like her." He glanced at Jakob. "Not like her at all," he repeated, as much to himself as to Jakob.

"You can't let your courtship end like that," Jakob said. "You've got to talk it out. Be sure the argument is about what you thought it was about."

"What?" Thomas said, pushing his hat back off his head.

"Be sure she's mad about what you think she's mad about. Women can be funny like that sometimes. They're complicated. You think she's upset about one thing when she's upset about another. You said yourself that her reaction didn't make sense. Talk to her."

"I don't know," Thomas hemmed. "I'm not sure she will even talk to me."

"Don't give up, I'm telling you. Don't take no for an answer," Jakob insisted. "You have to patch this up and go on with the wedding. You'll never be happy if you lose her, and I'd have to come up with a whole new plan to charm that little schoolteacher."

CHAPTER THIRTEEN

Leah, Sara and Ellie were clearing away the noon meal when Thomas drove his horse and open buggy into the yard. Hiram's dog barked, and Leah turned away from the window, her heart suddenly thudding in her chest. "It's Thomas," she said. "I don't want to see him."

"Don't want to see him?" Ellie repeated. "Have you two had a fight? I knew something was wrong." She cast a knowing look at Sara. "Didn't I tell you? Leah's been moping around for days."

Hiram jumped up from the table where he'd been finishing a second cup of coffee. "I got chores to do." Grabbing his hat from a hook on the wall, he hurried outside.

Leah put the dishes she'd carried from the table into the sink and untied her apron before turning to Sara. "I was waiting for a chance to tell you." She didn't make eye contact. "We've broken off the courtship. I can't marry Thomas."

Sara uttered a sound of exasperation. "If this is serious, you should have come to me. Why didn't you?"

"You aren't my mother," Leah said.

"No." Sara's mouth pursed in barely concealed pique. "I'm your matchmaker. You hired me to find the right husband for you. And if there is a problem —"

"I'm an adult. I don't have to explain to someone else why —" Leah broke off, suddenly mortified by the realization of how rude she sounded. "I'm sorry, Sara," she said, suddenly close to tears. "It's just that the reason we can't . . . It's personal. I didn't feel free to discuss it with anyone." She glanced out the window again. "He's coming. I can't talk to him." Running away might make her appear to be a foolish child, but she couldn't face him. "Please, Sara, I just can't —"

"Stuff and nonsense. Of course you'll speak to him. Whatever went wrong, we'll get to the bottom of it. Unless —" Sara's dark eyes narrowed. "Thomas didn't behave in —"

"*Ne*, nothing like that." Leah felt her cheeks grow hot with embarrassment. "Thomas would never attempt anything that would damage my honor — or his. He's a good man, the best, but —" She made a sound of distress. She didn't want to talk about this. She didn't want to think about it. "It's not Thomas that's the problem, Sara — it's me."

The screen door squeaked and Leah heard Thomas's footsteps on the porch.

"I've got mending to do," Ellie proclaimed before darting out of the kitchen.

Sara looked at Leah directly. "Sit down. Running away isn't the answer."

Leah felt light-headed. "I don't want to talk to him. There's nothing to say."

"Courtship is serious. You have every right to break it off. And so does Thomas," Sara said. "But there's a proper way to do it."

Leah slid into a kitchen chair. She had considered fleeing anyway, but she wasn't certain her legs would carry her. She wanted to cry. She felt so bad. Breaking up with Thomas had been the right thing to do. He deserved better. She just wasn't sure she could face him without bursting into tears again. This never would have happened if Sara had matched her with a settled older widower like she'd asked.

Leah heard footsteps and then Thomas's tall frame filled the doorway. He snatched off his hat, gripping it so hard between his fingers that it crumpled. "Leah. We have to

240

talk." His dark eyes were bloodshot, as if he hadn't slept. She could well understand that. She couldn't sleep, either. She felt sick.

"Sit down, Thomas." Sara rescued his hat and pushed a cup of coffee into his hands.

"Give me another chance," he said, staring at Leah. "I love you, Leah. I'll do whatever you want."

"Sit!" Sara pointed to a chair across from her. "Look at the two of you. Miserable as hens in a puddle. Long faces. And all because of a silly quarrel."

Thomas sat down hard. Leah felt his gaze on her, and she looked away and then down at her hands in her lap. Looking at him made it even harder to explain how she felt. She sat, hands laced together, knees trembling.

"I want to talk," he said. "That's all I was trying to do, to talk something out, but Leah thought I meant I'd made a decision and —"

"I overreacted," Leah blurted. "I did. But that's because . . ." She exhaled. "I can't marry Thomas. I just can't. I'm sorry I let it get this far. It was a mistake. I know that now."

"Leah, please," Thomas said. "You can't just walk away from me. What we have . . . what we've done together means something.

Whatever is wrong, we can fix it. I don't understand —"

"Exactly," she burst out. "You couldn't." She glanced at Sara, saw the disappointment and impatience in her eyes and found the strength to rise to her feet. "I respect you, Sara. You've been good to me, and I know you mean well, but I'm not right for Thomas and there's no sense in us talking about this. Find someone else for him. He deserves a good wife. It just can't be me."

With that, she walked away from him, out of the kitchen, and ran up the stairs to her bedroom. She closed the door behind her and went to the window, fighting tears. She leaned her face against the windowpane as waves of emotion surged through her. The sense of loss she'd felt when Daniel had died returned in full. "Help me," she prayed. "Please show me the way I should go."

Downstairs, Thomas looked at Sara. "What do I do now?" he asked. He got to his feet. "How do I fix this between us if I don't know what's wrong? If she won't even talk to me?" He shook his head. "The whole conversation was about whether or not we should consider being Mennonite instead of Amish. I never said that was what I wanted. I just wanted to talk to her about it. I wouldn't have brought it up if I'd known this would happen."

"I see." Sara nodded. "All right. So, in your heart of hearts, what would you rather do with your life? Would you rather remain in the Amish church or become Mennonite?"

"Amish. If it were my choice alone, there would be no question. I was only thinking of Leah and what she would have to give up." He gripped the back of a chair with one hand. "She's right. I don't understand." He scowled. "Was it so wrong of me to bring the question up to her?"

Sara scoffed. "Of course not. It's what couples do, certainly what married people should do. But I don't know that this is about religion. I think it could be about something more."

"That's what Jakob said." Thomas hung his head. "He said sometimes you think a woman is upset about one thing, when really it's about something else."

"Sounds likes Jakob knows something about women. At least relationships." She considered and then went on. "Go home and come back tomorrow. Leah may be willing to talk to you when she's calmed down."

"And if she doesn't?" he asked.

"I can't make her marry you, Thomas. If

you love her, if you truly believe that she is the one the Lord wants for you, then you have to have patience. You know that our Leah is headstrong. She likes to do things her way." A hint of a smile played over her lips. "Not unlike you, Thomas. But I think we can bring her around and get her past whatever made her react so badly to your attempt to talk to her about the Mennonite church." Her smile became a full one. "It wouldn't hurt to pray, not for what you want, but for what He thinks is best."

Thomas nodded and turned away. "I'm not going to give up on her," he said, feeling a little better with Sara's encouragement. Because he really did believe God meant Leah to be his wife. "Whatever I've done wrong, however I've hurt her, I'll make it right."

He carried that hope home with him and all the following day until he finished his work in the garden and returned to Sara's house. But there, standing on the front porch, once again, he was disappointed. "Leah still won't see me?" he asked Ellie.

"She isn't here. She went out after breakfast, and we haven't seen her all day."

Thomas stood there, feeling awkward, unsure what to do next. He wondered if he should try to find Leah, go from one sister's house to another asking for her. Anything was better than doing nothing.

"Thomas. I've been waiting for you." Sara came out of the house, dressed in her best church bonnet and black dress and cape. "Good, you came with your horse and buggy?"

"*Ya.*"

Ellie stepped into the house.

"I have an idea, but I can't do this on my own. I want you to drive me to Bishop Atlee's house. But first we have to stop and pick up Hannah."

"Why are we going to see the bishop? Is Leah at Hannah's?"

"Grace picked her up this morning on her way to the veterinarian clinic. But I doubt she took Leah to work with her. She's probably at Anna's or maybe Rebecca's. But before we can approach Leah, we have to get the bishop's approval. And her mother's." She took a deep breath. "Well, Thomas, what are you waiting for? Bring the horse around. We want to catch Bishop Atlee before he retires for his evening prayers."

Thomas held the door open for her. "I'll take you wherever you want to go, but why won't you tell me what you're planning to do? Surely, you aren't going to ask Bishop Atlee to try and convince her to marry me?"

"No sense in explaining my plan over and over," Sara said. "You'll find out soon enough." She folded her arms and regarded him sternly. "Now, are you in or not? Because if you've changed your mind about wanting to make Leah your wife, then this is a waste of time."

"Ne," he stammered. *"Ne.* You know I do."

Ellie came out of the house wearing her own black bonnet and dress cape. "Wait for me," she called.

"You're coming, too?" Thomas asked.

"Wouldn't miss it," Ellie said as she scrambled up into Thomas's buggy. "When Sara gets an idea, it will be too good to hear about secondhand." She looked at the dashboard. "I just hope you don't intend to turn on all these flashing blue lights tonight. It may not put the bishop in the best frame of mind to listen to what Sara has to say."

"Bishop Atlee has company," his wife said when Thomas knocked at his screen door. "But I'm sure he won't mind if all of you come in." She pushed open the door and welcomed them into her cheery kitchen.

Thomas waited for Sara, Hannah and Ellie to go first, then he entered, followed by gangly Irwin and his dog Jeremiah. Hannah had been just as puzzled and intrigued by Sara's invitation as Thomas had been. He hadn't expected Hannah's teenage foster son Irwin to climb into the buggy, as well.

"Ne." The bishop's wife pointed to the dog and shook her head. "Dogs stay outside."

Irwin, who'd been in the process of removing his straw hat, stopped short. "Jeremiah can't come in?"

"Your dog can stay on the porch," the woman said. "I'll even give him a nice bone I have left from our roast. But in my house, *ne.* Let me see how long he'll be." She held up one finger and disappeared down the hall. A moment later she was back. "Go on through. You know the way. My Atlee will be pleased to see you."

"If he has someone here, we can wait," Hannah offered.

"Atlee says you're to join him in the parlor," the bishop's wife insisted, stepping back to let them pass.

Irwin's plain face fell. "Guess I'll stay out here on the porch with Jeremiah," he said.

"Maybe I can find you an apple dumpling and a glass of milk," their hostess offered. "Growing boys are always hungry."

"Ya." Irwin nodded. *"Goot.* I like apple dumplings."

247

Thomas followed the women into the front room and was surprised to see Leah there ahead of him. "Leah?"

She rose from the bench where she'd been sitting across from the bishop. "Thomas?" Her cheeks reddened and she averted her eyes. "I didn't expect . . ." She glanced back at the church leader. "How did he know I was here?"

"We didn't," Sara said. "But it's best that you are. This will make my task easier." She nodded to the bishop. "Bishop Atlee." The others exchanged greetings.

"What a nice surprise." Atlee Borntrager chuckled and extended his arms. "Sit, sit, all of you. I'm very glad to have you in my home." He slid his thumbs under his suspenders. "First comes our Leah and now her young man, Thomas, with mother, friend and matchmaker. Mother!" he called to his wife. "Bring something cold to drink for our guests."

"I'll help her with the glasses," Ellie offered, slipping back out of the room.

Hannah and Sara settled themselves on a sofa that had seen better days. Thomas took a straight-backed wooden chair. He kept glancing at Leah, hoping she would favor him with a smile, but she didn't. She remained cool and formal.

248

"I'll get right to it, Bishop," Sara said. "As you know, these two, Leah and Thomas, have been walking out together."

He nodded and tugged unconsciously at his gray beard. "It's no news to me, Sara Yoder." He chuckled. "They're both taking my baptismal classes. Have you come to discuss the wedding plans?" he asked Thomas.

"Ne," Leah said. "There isn't going to be a wedding. Not between me and Thomas."

The older man looked at Leah thoughtfully. "Which is why you came to me, I suppose?"

She nodded.

"I think they've had a serious disagreement," Hannah explained. "We'd like to take every opportunity to help them work it out."

"Mam." Leah's eyes widened. "This is my affair. You shouldn't be involved."

"Why shouldn't I?" Hannah asked. "Who cares for you more than I do? I want you to be happy, with or without Thomas."

"Without," Leah said. "Definitely without."

"Is this a spiritual matter?" the bishop asked. "Something that I can be of help with?"

"What the two of them have is a lack of

249

communication," Sara said. "And *ya,* you can be of help. I've thought of a way that would improve their communication, but it will require your approval."

"I'm all ears," Bishop Atlee replied. He snapped one suspender against his dark blue shirt and crossed his ankles. Thomas noticed that he was in stockinged feet. One white sock had a neatly stitched patch on the heel.

The bishop's wife returned with tall glasses of homemade root beer. Ellie came after her carrying a plate of oatmeal cookies.

"What none of you seem to understand is that I can't marry Thomas," Leah said. "He's a good man. He'll make some woman a fine husband, but it can't be me. So there's no need for us to have better communication. Any communication."

"Did I tell you?" Hannah fussed. "Stubborn like her father. Always wanting to prove that she's right and everyone else is wrong."

Leah looked at Thomas. "I can't believe that you'd go along with this. You should know that what's between us is personal."

Bishop Atlee took a deep drink of his root beer and then set the mug down on the table beside his chair. "I, for one, would like to hear what Sara has to say. She's had a lot of experience in arranging marriages. And since we're all already here, I think we ought to listen to her."

"So do I," his wife agreed. "I think young couples are wise to listen to older heads. Marriage is a serious decision, not to be taken lightly." She squeezed in on the sofa beside Hannah. Ellie perched on a stool.

"Leah, Thomas, will you listen to my suggestion?" Sara asked.

Thomas nodded. "I brought you here, didn't I? I'm willing to try anything that will make things the way they were between me and Leah."

Leah twisted her hands in her lap.

She looked small and vulnerable to him. He wanted to take her in his arms and hold her against him. He wanted to smell the clean fragrance of her hair and feel her warm skin pressed to his. But she no longer wanted him, and he had to sit there, unable to comfort her.

Vaguely, he was aware of Sara saying something, but he was concentrating so hard on Leah that he didn't pay attention until he heard the bishop's wife give a gasp of astonishment.

". . . bundling was sometimes used in my community in Wisconsin. The couple —"

"Bundling?" Leah squeaked. "You want

me and Thomas to sleep in the same bed?"

That got Thomas's attention.

Sara spread her fingers in a calming motion. "Listen to me before you make up your mind. Bundling has always been a respected tradition among our people. True, you don't hear so much of it today, but it was done for many years in previous generations. Successfully."

"You're suggesting that Leah and Thomas do this?" Hannah asked.

Leah crossed her arms over her chest. "Absolutely not."

Bishop Atlee leaned forward in his chair. "Let's hear her out, Leah. I've heard that this is done in parts of Kentucky in some conservative communities. The bundling is well chaperoned, isn't it?"

"Usually by the girl's mother," Sara replied. "The couple is wrapped tightly and then sewn into separate blankets with a board between them so that they may not touch. A bed is set up in a common area, usually a parlor, and the prospective bride and groom spend the night together. A single candle lights the room, but the chaperone or chaperones remain awake. They keep a constant vigil to prevent any hint of impropriety."

"You're suggesting that you do this bundling at your home?" the bishop asked.

Sara shook her head. "I think her mother's home would be more appropriate. That is, if Hannah agrees."

Thomas swallowed. Spend the night in the same bed as Leah? Lie beside her in the darkness? He would agree to anything that would bring them together again, but there was no chance that Leah would do it.

"What would be the purpose?" Bishop Atlee asked. "In this instance? Wasn't it done with arranged marriages when couples didn't know each other?"

Sara nodded. "Sometimes. But the purpose is to provide a way for couples to get to know each other. It gives the man and woman privacy and the opportunity to talk in an intimate situation without the loss of reputation or morals." She looked from Thomas to Leah and back to the bishop. "I honestly believe that these two are perfect for each other. But they've hit an impasse. I think that confining the two of them to a bundling bed will ease the tension and let them discover how to communicate. Only by communicating can they get to the bottom of their disagreement."

The bishop looked at Hannah. "What would your husband think of such a proposal?"

"Albert?" Hannah considered. "He's a sensible man. Usually, he agrees with me in matters of my children. But I'd have to ask him."

Bishop Atlee nodded. "Do you approve of this scheme?" he asked Hannah.

"It doesn't matter whether she approves or not," Leah protested. She got to her feet. "I'm having no part of this. I can't believe that you'd ask me to do such a thing. And I know Thomas wouldn't —"

"Thomas wouldn't what?" He rose and extended a hand to her. "I would, Leah. I'd do anything to have you consent to be my wife. But . . . if I can't have you . . . then I think I deserve to know what I did wrong."

Leah wiped at her eyes. When she spoke, her voice was choked. "You didn't," she answered. "It's me. This is all my fault."

"You're scared," Ellie said.

"Scared?" Leah repeated. "That's not it at all."

"It is," Ellie insisted. "And Thomas is right. He deserves to know what went wrong between you."

"Spending the night sewn up in a blanket couldn't possibly change anything," Leah began.

"Maybe not," Thomas said. "But maybe it would. I think we should do it."

"Ne," she protested. "It's a waste of time. Nothing will be resolved."

Sara set her hands on her hips and met Leah's gaze. "Then what have you got to lose?"

CHAPTER FOURTEEN

"I can't believe that I've agreed to do this," Leah exclaimed. Three of her sisters were making up the bundling bed in her mother's front parlor and setting the room to rights for that evening. "This won't change anything," she insisted. "It will just make me feel stupid and give Thomas reason to hope that our relationship isn't over."

"I think it's old-fashioned," Miriam said as she tucked a corner of the sheet neatly under. "And a little odd. But if Sara, *Mam* and the bishop all think there's a reason for trying it, then I think you should go through with it. I trust them, and I know they only want what's best for you."

"I agree," Anna said. "Sara has had a lot of experience in matching couples. Why would she suggest this if she didn't think it was right? Besides, what's the worst that could happen? You could be right and all of us could be wrong. You love being right, Leah."

Leah glanced around at her sisters. It was impossible that they had all been won over by this absurd idea of Sara's. Why couldn't they see how much this was upsetting her? How could she bear to spend an entire night lying next to Thomas? It was wrong. It had to be. If it wasn't, why would she feel like this? "I think I'm sick," she said to Miriam. "I can't do it."

Miriam grimaced and threw her arms around her. "You'll be fine, baby sister. You're the tough one, remember? The one who went to the jungle and fought twenty-foot snakes and ate cannibal fish for Sunday breakfast."

"Be fine," Susanna echoed. She dropped the pillow she'd been stuffing into a pillowcase onto the mattress and came across the room to join in the hug.

"It wasn't twenty feet long," Leah protested. "It was seventeen. And I had to chase it away because it was trying to get through the window near the baby's bassinet."

"Exactly." Miriam chuckled.

Just the thought of her baby made her throat tighten. That loss ran so deep that she tried not to think about it. No mother should have to bury her child. And she shouldn't have to lay her precious baby in the ground when her husband lay close to death racked by the same tropical fever.

That day had been a nightmare. It was the rainy season in the Amazon. Water had poured from the skies, drenching her hair and clothing, filling the tiny grave with water. She'd wanted to go into the ground with her precious little one, but she couldn't allow herself to give up. God's strength had kept her upright and moving when she'd wanted to surrender. But she'd still had her husband to fight for, the man who had been the love of her life, the man she'd given up home and family to go with into the wilds of an unknown world to follow his dream.

Leah had shared that dream. She'd given herself wholeheartedly to ministering to the St. Joes and teaching in the one-room school. But hard work and good intentions hadn't been enough to protect them from the sorrows of the world. Sickness had come with the rains, devastating the villagers. When Daniel became ill, she'd prayed that he would survive the fever, but it ravaged his mind and body as swiftly as it had taken their beloved baby.

Two days, two long nights, and both were gone, lost to her on this earth. She would see them someday in heaven. She believed that with all her heart and soul, but *someday* stretched before her.

Close to tears, Leah went to the window and threw up the sash. She stared out at the green lawn and flowering shrubs that filled the air with a sweet and familiar scent, feeling lost even in her mother's home. She'd carried a seed of hope that here among her people she could find happiness and a new family, not to replace the dear ones that she had lost, but to help fill the emptiness inside her. Now she wondered if that had all been wistful thinking.

"Leah." Susanna stood beside her, tugging on her dress sleeve.

Normally, Leah would have gone out of her way to do anything for her sister, and she'd never ignore her. But Leah was so full of sorrow and grieving that she knew if she turned away from the window, she'd fall into a desolation of weeping. Crying always upset Susanna. And crying wasn't something that had been encouraged growing up in her mother's house.

"Save tears for the suffering of the long-ago martyrs," Hannah would say. She was always quick to kiss a scrape and hug a wailing child, but it was plain what was expected. "Stand tall, take your bumps and laugh at small injuries." No sissies under the Yoder roof. They came from a long line of strong women who'd faced death and torture to stand by their faith.

"Leah . . ." It was Susanna still.

"Leave her, sweetie," Anna said warmly. "Come on, Susanna, Miriam. We'll see what *Mam*'s up to in the kitchen. Sister needs some private time." Chattering, her sisters had all left her alone in the parlor.

Gratefully, Leah let her thoughts drift back to that small clearing in the jungle and the home she and Daniel had made out of a rough storage building with holes in the roof and vines climbing the inner walls. They'd learned to sleep in hammocks to avoid the ants and other biting insects that didn't fly, and she had done daily battle with biting flies, giant cockroaches, horned beetles and hungry mosquitoes.

They'd gone to serve a society of indigenous people where they were unwanted, and they had created a family of friends and faith. She'd been happy there at the mission with Daniel, so joyful in doing God's work, in bringing basic medical care and education to their community, that the hardships didn't matter. She'd been rich in everything that mattered, and she'd lost it in the space of hours.

Should she have come home at once? Would that have changed anything? Would she have gotten her grieving over quicker if she'd returned to Seven Poplars immediately after Daniel's death? But there had been no one to take her place. Villagers who she'd come to love and respect were ill and threatened by encroaching cattle ranchers and farmers who wanted to cut down the trees and build roads through the jungle, destroying the wildlife ecology and putting an end to the ancient way of life of the St. Joes. She'd been so busy, trying to do her job and fill Daniel's shoes that she hadn't had time to mourn or think of her loss. She'd risen before dawn and fallen into her hammock at night, exhausted. And, gradually, she'd found herself able to smile at a baby's laughter and found peace in the light of a glorious sunrise.

In time, perhaps, she would have found the satisfaction of her work that she'd known when Daniel was alive. Would she have remained there if the Mennonite committee had allowed it? She didn't know. She had put her trust in God that He knew what was best. And when the orders came for her to return to the States, she'd returned eager to wrap herself in the familiar scents and smells of home.

A mockingbird lit on a branch of the lilac bush near the window. Its song was so sweet

261

that Leah couldn't help but smile. Strange that the jungle, with its beautifully plumed birds didn't have one that Leah thought could compete in voice with the quiet tones of the mockingbird.

Her mother's voice cut through her reverie.

"Leah, look who's here."

She turned back to see her mother and Aunt Martha entering the parlor. Leah steeled herself to keep from showing her dismay at the visitor. Her aunt had always been a plain woman and the years since Leah had been away had taken their toll. Tall and thin as a garden rake with a tight mouth and small, deep-set eyes, Aunt Martha always gave the appearance of a woman who smelled something distasteful on someone's shoe and was searching for the source.

"Leah, dear," her aunt said. "I'm shocked that you would consider such a thing. I told your uncle, I'll just march over there and have a word with Hannah. To think that she'd condone bundling under her own roof. No one does it anymore. At least not here. Maybe in one of those backward communities in the Western states. But it just isn't done among the pious. I wanted you to know that you're putting your reputation in jeopardy by spending the night with this runabout ruffian."

"Thomas is hardly a ruffian," Leah defended.

"Bishop Atlee has allowed it," her mother said. Leah could tell that her mother was fighting her amusement. Often, it was either laugh at Aunt Martha or be vexed by her interfering behavior. Usually, Hannah chose laughter.

"Humph." Aunt Martha sniffed. "Very odd. But Hannah's daughters have always had her stubborn nature. If you're determined to go through with this, it's my duty to make sure that no high jinks take place. I told your mother that I'd sit up with her tonight, just to make sure."

Leah gritted her teeth. "That's kind of you, Aunt Martha, but there's no need. *Mam* will have Sara with her. And, of course, Albert."

"Your stepfather. Practically a stranger to you." She picked up the corner of the beautiful quilt that Ruth had made and examined the stitching before wrinkling her nose in distain. "And him fast asleep upstairs in his bed, no doubt. I know men and the good they would be in such a situation." She dropped the quilt, sighed as if to dismiss the needlework and smoothed it out. "No, indeed. Sara or no Sara, I'm staying. I want no one pointing fingers at you and whispering behind your back. A young widow must guard her reputation. What if you spend the night with Thomas and he still refuses to marry you? What then?"

"I'm not marrying Thomas," Leah said.

Aunt Martha gasped. "Then why are you sleeping with him?"

"To prove a point," Leah answered. "And to satisfy Sara and my family."

"And you won't be deterred from this nonsense?" Aunt Martha huffed.

"*Ne,* Aunt. I won't."

Standing slightly behind Aunt Martha and out of her line of sight, Hannah shrugged and gave a helpless expression. "I suppose, if you insist on staying, Martha, I won't turn you out of my house."

"I should think not. This is my late brother's house. And I remember him if others don't." Her aunt lifted the top quilt and inspected the wooden barrier that ran from the headboard to the footboard and divided the two sides of the bed. "And where did you find this?" she asked, rapping on the wood with her fist. "I wouldn't imagine that you had a bundling board tucked up in the attic."

"Sara asked James to make it for her," her mother explained. "She gave him the specifications. Who knows, if this works, it may catch on in Seven Poplars."

"Adequate, I suppose." Aunt Martha sighed heavily, ignoring Hannah's jest. "But I still believe you're wrong to agree to it. You'll regret it or she will. Mark my words."

For once she's right, Leah thought. *I regret it already.*

Leah closed her eyes and counted to three hundred. Thomas didn't say a word but she could hear him breathing, slow even breaths. It was unnerving. The sheets that were sewn tightly, making a cocoon around her body, the wooden board that ran the length of the bed, and the light of the single candle did little to allay her nervousness.

Thomas was lying inches from her in the semidarkness. They were supposed to be talking. Communicating. But he hadn't said anything. Goose bumps rose on her arms and the back of her neck. She was alternately too hot and then chilled. This was unnatural. There was a man in her bed and he wasn't her husband, and there were four people on the other side of the closed door. Custom aside, the bishop's permission aside, it was unnerving. It didn't matter that they were both fully dressed from head to toe; this felt more intimate than the days and evenings they'd spent driving in her car or walking on the boardwalk in Rehoboth.

She lay perfectly still, afraid to move, not knowing what he'd do or say if she did move. Her own breathing seemed too fast, too erratic. Her heart raced. She wanted to call out to her mother or to Sara and tell them that this was a huge mistake. She wanted out. She wanted to be away from Thomas and this farce of a courtship. But Aunt Martha was here in the house. If she weakened, her aunt would seize on it. She would know that she'd been talked into something that she couldn't fulfill. She would appear weak and vulnerable.

Weakness was ammunition you never wanted to give Aunt Martha. Like a bullying hen who rules the chicken run with pointy beak and sharp claws, her aunt would seize any weakness and take advantage of it. Worse, she would spread the news far and wide that Hannah's Mennonite daughter wasn't as much as she thought she was.

Not that she cared so much what Aunt Martha thought of her. Aunt Martha had never been fond of Hannah or of her and her sisters. But weakness would also make Hannah look bad. It would give Aunt Martha pleasure in some twisted kind of way

266

that wasn't Amish at all. And she didn't want to do anything that would make her mother look bad. She couldn't. She owed her that much. So Leah would stick this out. She'd be here in the morning, just as determined not to wed Thomas as she was at this moment. She'd do it if it killed her.

So why wasn't he saying anything? Had he realized how useless this whole fiasco was and simply gone to sleep? Could he sleep wrapped up as tight as a cured ham? And if he could, what did that say about all his protests that he loved her? It was demeaning, really. According to Sara, she and Thomas were supposed to communicate. They were supposed to exchange thoughts and hopes. At least, that's what Sara had said.

But Sara was wrong. As were her mother and the bishop and most of her sisters. Susanna didn't really understand what was happening. She'd thought it was funny when Sara had stitched her up in the sheet, and she'd giggled loudly when Mam did the same for Thomas. Her husband David, who'd followed her into the parlor, had chuckled, too.

"Time you two were abed, as well," her mother had said to Susanna. "Tomorrow is library day, and you and David will have to be up early to watch for book borrowers."

"Ya," Susanna agreed. Her eyes sparkled with excitement. "Librar-ry day." And then, as she'd been leaving, she'd giggled and wagged a chubby finger at Leah and Thomas. "No kissing!" she admonished. "Only married kissing."

Kissing. Leah grimaced. That was the last thing on her mind. "Thomas," Leah whispered. "Are you awake?"

No answer.

"Thomas?" He had to be asleep. How insulting. What suitor would agree to bundling with his intended and then go to sleep? She wriggled, trying to get more comfortable. She wasn't used to lying down with her prayer covering on and she knew it had fallen down out of place, but she couldn't get her hands loose to adjust it. "Thomas?" she repeated.

"Tell me about Daniel." His voice seem to float in the air.

"What did you say?" she asked.

"He must have been a special person. Tell me about him and your life together at the mission."

"He was special. He was everything to me. Daniel . . ." She trailed off as tears flooded her eyes. "I don't want to talk about Daniel."

"Why not?" Thomas's voice was low, but she could hear every word he uttered. "When you talk about Daniel, you honor him."

"I don't feel like I'm honoring him." She swallowed. Tears ran down her cheeks. She struggled to get an arm free and heard the tiny rip as threads pulled loose. Immediately, she lay perfectly still. Had Thomas heard the threads tearing? Sara had sewn these seams. She was an excellent needle-woman. Her stitching shouldn't have come undone.

"Why would you say such a thing, Leah?" His voice was warm and gentle. "What do you think you've done wrong? If you had died instead of Daniel, would you have expected him to live alone for the rest of his life? Is that what he wanted for you?"

If Thomas had raised his voice or if he'd insisted that she answer him, she could have stood firm. But the tender cadence of his question touched something deep within her. *"Ne,"* she whispered. "The last thing he said to me was to remarry and have more children."

"He must have loved you very much."

Grief so powerful that she was helpless against it swept over her. She cried softly, as she remembered Daniel's insistence that she live for both of them. Thomas said nothing, but she could feel his nearness. And then, as her sobs subsided, she began to relate incidents of her life with Daniel, some funny, others solemn or poignant. And once she'd begun to talk, the words spilled out of her.

She talked for what seemed like hours and in that span of time, she gradually loosened the stitches in her sheet so that her left arm and hand were free so that she could wipe her eyes or scratch her nose when it itched. A nagging guilt told her that getting partially out of the sheet might be against the rules, but it wasn't as if she meant to do anything wrong. Was it her fault if Sara had used old thread?

Thomas rarely interrupted as she spoke. Sometimes, if the tale she was telling was amusing, he would chuckle, or sometimes he would comment briefly, but mostly, he listened.

Now and then, the parlor door would open and the beam of a flashlight would pass over them. Leah would hear her mother's murmur or her aunt's brusque tone or Sara's matter-of-fact statement, "All is as it should be." And then the door would squeak closed, and she and Thomas would be left alone again.

Sometime after the midnight chime from the grandfather clock, the breeze through the open window caught the flame of the candle. The candle sputtered and then went out, leaving them in total darkness except for the moonlight that spilled into the room.

She had just finished telling Thomas about the time she and Daniel and two of the St. Joes had gone on a fishing trip on the river and gotten caught in a thunderstorm, when Thomas abruptly spoke up.

"I'm sorry I upset you so much by bringing up the subject of me becoming Mennonite instead of you joining the Amish church."

"I thought you knew how much I wanted to be Amish again."

"I thought that you had made the decision so that you could be one with your family again," Thomas said. "I didn't realize how important it was to you."

"I see that now," she said, "but I would never have believed that you would waver in your faith."

"It was for you," he said. "I didn't want you to sacrifice your religion for me. Besides, your faith didn't waiver when you became Mennonite for Daniel." He exhaled. "I just wanted to talk about it."

"And I wouldn't listen," she whispered.

"That was wrong of me. You had the right . . . *have* the right to decide for yourself. Not everyone is called to our faith."

"For myself, I'd never walk away. I was born Amish and I'd die Amish. But I'd do anything for you, Leah."

"So you don't want to be Mennonite?"

"Nope."

"Not even for the convenience of the car?"

He chuckled. "Nope."

She lay there in the darkness, wondering how she could have hurt him so thoughtlessly. Why had they never talked like this before? Things could have been so different.

"I wondered," Thomas mused. "Is it the same? When you're sitting in a Mennonite church service, do the hymns lift your heart in the same way?"

"They do." She found herself smiling in the darkness. "When Daniel asked me to marry him and I decided to become Mennonite for him, it seemed an easy decision. With him and in our home, it was easy. But outside, among other members of the church, it always felt like a new pair of shoes — useful, handsome, but not quite as comfortable as my old, worn pair." She exhaled softly. "I never told Daniel that."

"*Ne,* you didn't want to burden him with

the thought that he had led you away from something you loved."

"If he'd lived, I never would have thought of returning to the Amish faith. But after he died, I prayed about it every night. I asked God to show me His plan for me. I put my life in His hands, and He led me back home. It's why I can't bear the thought of changing again. In my heart, I'm already Amish," she admitted.

"You won't miss driving the car or the freedom you've had?"

"I don't think I will. It's not giving up the world — it's embracing something more real. I want to marry, to have more children, and to raise them in the faith I grew up in. I want that peace for them."

"You could have just said that," Thomas said. "You didn't have to become so emotional, to start an argument with me. You didn't have to break off our courtship because I asked a question about our future."

"Ne," she admitted. "I didn't." And then, suddenly, the truth was as clear as day to her. About what had happened that night on the walk. After the kiss they had shared. The kiss she had enjoyed very much. "I don't think it was so much what you said, Thomas. I think . . . I think I was looking

for a reason to break it off with you."

"Because you don't love me?"

"Because I do, Thomas. Don't you see?" Sobs shook her body, making it hard to speak. "Daniel was the love of my life. So how can I love you? How can my heart skip a beat when I see you walking toward me across the field? How can I feel such longing to have you kiss me?"

"But you meant to marry. You asked Sara to find you a husband."

"A husband," she repeated. "Someone I could respect, a companion, a father for my children. I never thought she'd find me a man I could love. Because loving you feels like betraying Daniel."

"Did your mother love your father?" Thomas asked.

"Of course she did," Leah answered.

"And does she love Albert?"

"*Ya,* of course. But not like she loved *Dat.*"

"How do you know what's in her heart? And if she does love Albert every bit as much, do you blame her?"

"*Ne,*" Leah insisted.

"So if Hannah's loving Albert isn't wrong, then you loving me can't be, either. You aren't betraying Daniel," Thomas said. "You're fulfilling your promise. Living for him, living for both of you. And if you believe God led you home to Seven Poplars, can't you believe He led you to me, as well?"

"Oh, Thomas." She sat upright, tearing out the stitching that confined her left side. She reached over the bundling board to touch his face, just as his arms came around her. "Thomas?"

He sat up and pulled her against him.

"How did you?" she began. "My mother's stitching shouldn't have torn out."

"Not unless she intended it to," he answered, smoothing her hair. "I suspect neither Hannah nor Sara intended us to remain apart all night."

Leah shivered as his warm lips fit perfectly to hers and they kissed, a kiss so sweet and tender that she didn't want it to end. "I love you," she murmured. "Love you, love you." She gazed into his eyes, their noses touching.

"Enough to become my wife?" he asked breathlessly.

"Can we be married as soon as we're baptized?"

"As soon as Bishop Atlee gives his blessing."

"Then, yes, Thomas, I will marry you."

He kissed her again, and she wasn't sure if she would have had a third kiss if the door hadn't opened and her aunt Martha hadn't shrieked, "Sara! Hannah! Come quick! The fox is in the henhouse!"

EPILOGUE

One year later . . .

Leah parked next to a Do Not Litter sign
and turned off the ignition. It was early
morning, and the sky was just beginning to
fade from dark to light. They were close
enough to the shoreline that she could hear
the ocean waves through the open windows
of the vintage black truck. Around them, in
the scrubby salt pines, birds were coming
awake, and rabbits and mice were beginning to stir.

Thomas walked around the truck and
opened the driver's door. Leah turned
toward him and he caught her by the waist
to lift her down to the ground. "Wait," she
said. "Let me take off my shoes."

"Let me, *leibschdi.*"

Sweetheart. Her throat clenched at the
endearment.

Tenderly, Thomas untied her sneakers and
removed them one at a time. After each

shoe slid off into his hand, he set it back inside the truck and tenderly massaged each of her feet, taking care to concentrate on her sensitive arches and toes.

"That tickles," she teased, but she liked it. She loved the feel of Thomas's hands, so strong and yet so gentle. When he stepped back, she slid down off the seat. The surface of the parking lot was pleasantly cool on her feet. "Better take off your shoes, as well. Sand in them won't be fun."

"*Ne,* I suppose it wouldn't." He tugged off his boots and socks and tossed them into the back of the truck.

They had been up for hours, loading the truck and driving south from Seven Poplars. After some persuasion on Leah's part, Bishop Atlee had decided to allow her to own a motor vehicle. The rules were that she could drive to deliver Thomas's organic fruits and vegetables to the restaurants and to take community members to doctor and dentist visits. It was a trial period, which the elders could extend, so long as Leah and Thomas used the horse and buggy at home and didn't use the vehicle for personal use.

She had traded the little black car for an old black truck with a reliable motor. Their first delivery today was in Ocean City, across the state line into Maryland, but it was early yet, and Thomas had wanted to take the time to stop and see the sunrise over the ocean.

"I hope we won't be late," she said. "New customers and —"

"We won't be late," he answered. And taking her hand, he led her away from the truck and down the wooded path to the beach. The boardwalk gave way to hard-packed sand, and the smell of the sea blended with the spicy scent of pine needles. Here, it was still night, and the trees loomed black against charcoal foliage. But the sound of the surf was louder now, and Leah's heartbeat quickened in anticipation.

They traversed another bend in the trail and Thomas held a pine branch up so that she could duck under it. Suddenly, they were out of the dunes and onto the beach. It stretched out on either side of them, with the ocean directly ahead and filling the horizon.

Shorebirds were there ahead of them at the water's edge. Long-legged shadows darted back and forth on the sand, bobbing rhythmically as they searched the wet sand for the ocean's bounty. Noisy gulls flapped and dove overhead. From behind them, Leah heard the hoarse cry and the muffled flapping of a blue egret's wings.

The ocean was a dark mass, lit now by rays of iridescent light. Clouds piled one upon another, pink and peach and lavender, and shining through, seemingly borne of the surface of the waves, came the glory of the sun. Leah stopped short, made speechless by the beauty of the sunrise. Thomas let go of her hand and slipped an arm around her shoulder. For minutes, they stood there, watching, mesmerized as dawn banished the darkness. Leah swallowed against the constriction in her throat and blinked back tears. "Wonderful," she whispered.

"It is, isn't it?" Thomas answered. "Whenever I see a sunrise, over the water here or the fields at home, it makes me think of God's love for us."

"*Ya,*" she agreed. "Me, too."

"I think the beauty of a sunrise is here to tell us that love is like the light," Thomas said. "You can't measure it out in cups or bushels. It just is, and it is eternal."

"Sometimes, I think you would make a good preacher."

"Me?" Thomas snorted. "Hardly."

"You have a deep core of wisdom," she confided. "You understood what I didn't." She leaned against him, pressing her face against his chest. "Thank you for bringing me here to see it."

"You're part of it," he said. "Part of the beauty."

She chuckled. "Hush, you shouldn't say that. You'll make me guilty of *hockmut.*"

"Leah, you are a woman with more reason than most to feel pride in her appearance, and yet you show it least." He smiled down at her. "I doubt very much that the bishop will be admonishing you for showing pride."

She slipped her arms around his neck and stood on tiptoe. He bent and their lips met. His mouth was sweet and she thrilled to the sensation. "You will lead me into wicked thoughts," she teased.

"I might. I never made any bones about the fact that I liked to have fun. And two people who love each other are sometimes tempted to play."

"But temptation doesn't always have to win out." Laughing, she whirled away from him and ran through the sand to the water's edge. Waves were breaking close to shore and salt water foamed and washed around her ankles.

"Watch out. You'll get caught in one and end up wet to the neck," Thomas warned.

In answer, she caught up her skirts and waded deeper into the water. It was cool and invigorating. She felt like a child again, playing tag with the waves. Venturing out, only to run for the beach when a larger wave threatened.

"Be careful," Thomas said.

Another waved crashed around her, splashing salt water to her knees. "Come try it!" she dared.

Thomas looked up and down the beach. Leah did the same. The only living thing she could see was a sand flea digging out of the hard-packed sand, a line of fiddler crabs and the birds.

"Chicken!" she cried.

"Really? We'll see who's chicken." Thomas pushed down his suspenders and stepped out of his trousers, leaving him clad only in his shirt and one-piece white cotton under-garment. It was sewn of heavy white cotton and consisted of a short-sleeved undershirt and drawers that came down halfway to his knees. English men wore much less when they went into the water. All the same, it was hardly an exhibition that the elders would approve of by a baptized member of the church, even on a swimming beach.

"You wouldn't," she said, suddenly not so certain what he would or wouldn't do. She was so busy watching Thomas that she forgot to watch the ocean. A big wave rolled in, drenching her halfway to the waist and nearly knocking her off her feet.

Thomas doubled up with laughter.

"Not funny!" she shouted back, although it was funny.

But what was he up to now? Leah gaped in surprise as Thomas removed his shirt, folded it and laid it on the sand and put his hat carefully on top of it. "Thomas . . ."

Wearing only his undergarment, he dashed down the beach, splashed past her and dove into the water. He swam out to where the waves were breaking. A wave crashed over Thomas, and Leah lost sight of him. Fearful for his safety, she pulled up her skirt and waded deeper. Water wet her up to her thighs.

"Thomas!" She was about to go in after him when he bobbed up, laughing, a few yards away. Thomas had never told her that he could swim like a fish.

"Come in." He gestured to her.

Leah backed toward the shore. "I don't think so."

"Maybe I'll catch you and throw you in." He got to his feet and moved toward her, but she fled to the beach. He followed and caught up with her on the sand.

He wrapped his dripping arms around her and kissed her. "I love you," he said.

"And I love you," she replied. He was wetter than she was, but she didn't care. The warmth of the rising sun enveloped them both, and she clung to him as he kissed her again.

"Are you happy?" he asked her. "Have I made you happy?"

She looked up into his dark eyes. "And why wouldn't I be happy?" she murmured. "You've given me everything that I could want — a home, work that I love, a future."

He nuzzled the crown of her head. "I think I could have coaxed the skirt off you," he teased. "You'd make a beautiful mermaid."

"My skirt, maybe," she replied. "But not my shift or my scarf."

He chuckled, but then she felt his muscles tense and his tone grew serious. "You're not sorry you married me, are you, Leah?"

"This would be a fine time to decide that," she answered. "And me, a respectable Amish wife, alone with a half-dressed man on a deserted beach."

"Your half-dressed *husband,*" he corrected.

She laughed and stepped away, smoothing down her wet skirt and shaking out some of the sand. He reached out and cupped her rounded tummy in his big hand. Shyly, she covered his hand with her own. "Soon, I'll be so fat that you could roll me down to the beach," she whispered.

"I don't care how fat you get," he said, leaning down to speak to the little one growing under her heart. "I love this little one more than fried chicken and dumplings. And you will, too."

"We'll have no chicken or dumplings if we don't get those vegetables delivered," Leah reminded him. Her hand rested protectively on her belly. "You said we were coming to look at the ocean sunrise."

"And we did, didn't we?" Thomas grinned at her as he went to retrieve his clothing. "Life isn't all work. Sometimes you need to stop a moment and just enjoy it."

"I do," she said. "Every day, living with you, being your wife." How could she explain the joy he'd brought her? It was a new beginning. Life with Thomas was different than life with Daniel, but it was no less fulfilling.

Together, they were building a new house, building the farm and planning for the child that would be born to them in the late fall. "Have you thought what you'll name the baby, if it's a girl?" she asked as he dressed. He'd let her pick a boy's name, and she'd chosen Jonas, after her father.

He pushed back his damp hair and settled his straw hat on his head. "I'm thinking either Hannah or Martha," he teased.

"Martha?" she cried. "You wouldn't do that to our innocent baby, would you?"

"Well," he explained as he led the way back to the truck, "that might get us back in your aunt Martha's good favor."

"Good try," she answered. "But nothing would keep us there long. You have to remember that I'm one of Hannah's girls."

"Fair enough," Thomas said with a grin. "Then Hannah it will have to be."

Laughing, they climbed back into the truck and Leah backed out of the parking space and pulled carefully back onto Coastal Highway. "Hannah Stutzman," she murmured. "It has a nice ring to it, doesn't it?"

"It does," Thomas agreed. "But not nearly as *goot* as Leah Stutzman."

"Oh, Thomas, what a thing to say. What will our baby think if she hears you?"

"She'll think that her *dat* is head over heels for her *mam*. And what's wrong with that? Besides, it's going to be a boy. Jonas. A good name for a farmer."

"Or a blacksmith," she teased.

"Or a blacksmith. Whatever he wants to do for a living will be fine with me, so long as he remembers that all blessings come from a merciful God."

Leah could add nothing to that. And when Thomas began to hum and then to sing a joyful hymn as they rolled along, she joined in with him. Together they sang the old beloved verses of a song they had learned as children as they drove into the bright, sunny morning, full of hope for whatever lay ahead.

Dear Reader,

A first love is always a special life experience, but sometimes life doesn't turn out the way we expect. In *A Love for Leah* we see what happens when matchmaker Sara Yoder tries to arrange a second chance at love for a young widow who many of our readers may remember fondly, Hannah's daughter Leah. Seeking to heal from the tragic loss of her young family while on mission in the Amazon rainforest, she believes she can find peace and a new start in the traditional Amish community of Seven Poplars.

Leah wants desperately to have another child, so she asks Sara to arrange a marriage of convenience with an older man. Leah believes she will be content with a quiet partnership built on faith and respect. She never expects to become reacquainted with handsome, vivacious Thomas, or to fall head over heels in love with him. And when she does, her heart is torn. Will marrying Thomas for love rather than convenience be a betrayal to her first husband? Will this be a match that Sara can't manage?

I hope that you'll enjoy Leah's journey in search of happiness. I'm always glad to welcome readers old and new to stories of love and life among the Amish.

Wishing you peace and joy,

Emma Miller

ABOUT THE AUTHOR

Emma Miller lives quietly in her old farmhouse in rural Delaware. Fortunate enough to be born into a family of strong faith, she grew up on a dairy farm, surrounded by loving parents, siblings, grandparents, aunts, uncles and cousins. Emma was educated in local schools and once taught in an Amish schoolhouse. When she's not caring for her large family, reading and writing are her favorite pastimes.

The employees of Thorndike Press hope you have enjoyed this Large Print book. All our Thorndike, Wheeler, and Kennebec Large Print titles are designed for easy reading, and all our books are made to last. Other Thorndike Press Large Print books are available at your library, through selected bookstores, or directly from us.

For information about titles, please call:
(800) 223-1244

or visit our website at:
gale.com/thorndike

To share your comments, please write:
Publisher
Thorndike Press
10 Water St., Suite 310
Waterville, ME 04901

DUE

18